The Laird & Lady
Series

CW00482281

Comparisons and Opposites
Book 6

By
Barbara Raw

Coming Home

The village bells in Dunvegan toll.

"My Laird, tis yer son from Urquart! He's wi ten men." A guard informed Laird MacLoud.

"Och, he's returned te visit us Meredith!"

"Really? Elford's here?" Lady Meredith asked.

"Aye love, tis our youngest, he's come home."

Lady Meredith rushed up to the battlements of the castle where she knew she'd have the best view of any visitors. Husband Laird Stefan is hot in her footsteps.

"Oh Lord, just look at him! He's sitting so tall! Six months away from us and he's returned. Looks like a king sat there and who is that horse?"

"Och will ye look at tha? Tis Urquod love, mi Black's first foal. Tis a grand sight indeed. Come on, let's go doon n' meet him."

Six months earlier, since twins Dolan and Elford, sons to Laird Stefan MacLoud of Dunvegan on Skye. had completed their years of Laird ship training, since being eight summers in age. Dolan the eldest son by just minutes, shall take his father's seat when he steps down at Dunvegan Castle. Elford the younger, is set to become Laird of Urquart Castle although he shall have a further three years of training upon arrival and when the current Laird Kenneth steps down.

Both boys look just like their father Stefan. All muscle, broad shouldered, dark hair, and even darker eyes, both have brawn and devilishly good looks. Pure warriors of Scotland.

Dolan is known for being the slightly more sensible twin, whereas Elford, takes a few more risks and is fond of the ladies.

The young men have sat alongside their father now many times within almost all of his duties, such as council meetings, advisories, and tedious audiences with petty village squabbles among neighbouring farmers. They had been allowed to settle many problems as their father sat back and listened to their reasoning and judgement. If he deemed them unfair, he would step in and suggest a better way to resolve the situation or meet halfway.

The time had come for Elford to leave Castle Dunvegan for Urquart and his additional years of training. As the family wave him off, Elford is excited to start a new adventure in his life. If he knuckled down for a while longer, he'll make a good Laird and will earn the respect of the village folk.

Rekindled Love

Tina is Seelie Fae and pure of heart. She was set forever young by Danu, the Goddess of all Fae, at twenty-one summers. Her husband is Colby, Man at Arms and Second in Command to the Laird MacLoud. They grew up together as boys when his parents were lost in a battle or, so it was presumed. Colby had tagged along with a small group of local lads and ended up within the castle walls for safety. He stayed and rose through the ranks alongside Stefan as the years went by. Now, Stefan trusts him with his life, he is his equal.

Tina and Colby have been trying for a family for some time since they were wed. She was once with child but after a severe fever from rat bites, she lost the bairn and hasn't been able to conceive since. Eventually Tina had recovered but now she cannot stand the thought of being alone without Colby or any of her friends that are alive now. She wishes to age alongside them, and this caused quite a few arguments. Colby didn't want her to die at any time, he wished for her to have a long life, an immortal life that she was given the gift of.

Lady Mary MacLoud is Stefan's Mother, is resting again. She's been very tired of late, to the point where Stefan and Meredith, his wife, call the Healer in to check on her. The Healer says she is healthy for her age, just tired and needs lots of rest. Some older folks do, it's like a hibernation in winter, the darker colder months. It might do her good!

Mary dreams every night about visiting the Tween Realm again. She had been there before, many years ago when she escaped from an Unseelie army in the battle of Fingal's Cave. Also, when her sister Hanna passed and she managed to catch her to say her goodbyes within the Tween.

Laird Stefan had been running a Horse Breeding Programme for some years now, using his own horse, the Black – a War Horse and a stallion. He'd sired many mares and had produced some mighty fine offspring, but his first-born foal is special to the Laird. His name is Urquod whom at the time, was a smaller version of his sire, jet black, with a prancing proud gait that all the other foals followed.

Nicholas was the Man in Charge of the Breeding Programme. His wife Isla is a former Ladies Maid within the castle, and they now live together and have their own chambers as part of the Laird's family.

Urquod is now nine summers old and is a huge stunning

black stallion. Laird Kenneth of Urquart had offered Stefan a high sum of coinage to buy him. Stefan refused but when the village was hit with Ergotism, the foods were all destroyed as it poisoned folk along with their livestock. Everything had to be burned. Laird Urquart had come and helped them by supplying food to carry on and seed grain to allow them to plant more and be able to survive the coming winter. He was the man who saved the village folk from starving with his generosity and kindness. Stefan had agreed to allow him to take Urquod home with him. It was sad to watch him prance off as he left Dunvegan Castle but the alliance with Urquart is really strong, he knew he would be in good hands, and he was proud that another Laird was very pleased with his work.

A Forge with a small house aside it, had been built within the walls of Dunvegan and a new position of Blacksmith had been offered. As word spread, a man called Angus MacDerum was successful in his bid to accept it. The Laird had selected him from a few men that had come forward and his work was the best suited for Stefan's needs. His forging skills were stunning. Angus also brought two beautiful daughters with him. Harriet and Maisie, although he had no wife. She had perished with an illness some years ago and Angus has practically reared the girls himself.

Lady Meredith MacLoud adores Stefan still, their love and

respect for each other over the years has grown stronger and stronger. She'd gone through a difficult time these last few years especially when she took an arrow to the stomach and lost her unborn child. It almost ended her life, but she recovered. Then she hit the menopause early due to having her womb removed by an old Seer named Helga, who is a good friend of the family. In doing this Helga had saved her life, but there would be no more children. Stefan had taken Meredith away for a few days camping at Fancy Hill, a marvellous place with stunning scenery and many flowering plants, it had done the pair of them so much good. Their love had been rekindled and awakened. Meredith sleeps better now that she has learned to cope with nightly flushes, mood swings and sudden sweats. The Healer's had helped her through and had advised her to talk to her husband, she did, and he listened and heard her. It made all the difference in their lives and Stefan was there to fully support her through.

Kaylee a dwarf Seelie Fae, set forever young at fifteen summers hand become hand fast to Ghilly, a male dwarf Fae set at twenty-one summers. There are both very good friends of the clan and live close by in the Orchard House at Dunvegan village. They tend the fruit and vegetable fields, then take them to the castle to exchange for pies, breads, and puddings. Other folk in the village also barter their goods, the Laird had once offered them coin for it, but they had no need of coin, nothing to buy and had kindly refused his offer. Kaylee had Fae abilities, one of them being visions, where she can look into greying mists and see future events, locate people and recognise scenery. It's proved useful in the past. She also has talents surrounding animals and it seems she has a way to communicate easily with them. She has a Wolfhound named Janson who she sometimes rides alongside Hawk, a bird of prey. Kaylee did have two hounds, but when Ergotism hit the village some time back, Sharoc, the other hound, had become very ill and he died in her arms. She still misses him today and thinks of him often. She also has a stocky skewbald pony named Prudence who is really good and very patient with foals.

Years ago, the Mother Goddess of all Fae, Danu, had allowed four Seelie Fae to live and reside in the deep forests of Scotland. After a time, their Fae abilities combined caused a few problems, so they all went their separate ways. To the mountains, the caves and other forests but one had joined the dark Unseelie Fae and had later perished in fight near Eilean Donan. Three others are still alive, Tina, Kaylee, and Aria.

Aria is also fifteen summers and set forever young, she's a wonderful artist, especially with oil paints and had painted a large image a while back of Urquart Castle, the Laird Kenneth loved it and Stefan had asked her to paint one of Dunvegan too. She once lived in the Orchard House with Kaylee, but as Ghilly came along, she felt a little pushed out, a gooseberry of sort and had gone to live with Helga on the shores of Loch Ness. Helga often needed a hand and welcomed her into her home. She continues to teach her things that may help her live easier in the future. Helga herself seems to have some kind of Fae ability even though she's an elderly lady, she doesn't seem to age anymore though either, but they both adore their new cat, Mr Tibs. Ghilly had brought Aria him when he'd been to a local village trading point and thought she'd like him. She did, greatly

Unchaperoned

Laird Stefan held his wife's hand as they ploughed down the stone trod to meet their son Elford, whose returning after six months of training at Urquart Castle. Although Stefan is tall, strong, and very handsome, he's had his fair share of battle wounds and broken bones. On the coldest days in Skye, he found his bones stiffening, but he'd never let on or admit it.

"Mother, Father, I've missed ye!" Elford said as he dismounted Urquod.

Colby, Stefan's Man at Arms came to hold the reins as Elford hugged his parents.

"Just look at Urquod love, he's a mighty fine horse Elford, ye treating him well."

"Aye father, he's a looker alreet, a tad frisky wi the ladies though, just like mi, eh?"

Lady Meredith gently slapped Elford on the shoulder, scolding his coarseness.

"Come in son, refreshments now, then we'll feast laters. Colby, can ye let Anna ken, the maids fer the chambers and ave the lads fetch more logs please?" Colby handed Urquod's reins to Nicholas, who led him to the stalls.

"Reet away My Laird."

"Och whose tha father?" Elford asked.

"Who, the woman at the Forge?"

"Aye, the bonnie red head Da?"

"She's one of our new Blacksmith's daughter's son, he has two, both equally as bonnie."

"Er, you two, do you mind? When you've done ogling all the lasses, I'd like to chat with my son!" Meredith added.

The group of ten guards who had accompanied Elford, also entered the main hall. Laird Stefan and Lady Meredith took their seats on the dais as their sons sat either side of them, followed by Caitlin, their twelve summers old daughter. Other men and women sat a little further down on wooden benches with long tables which maids were filling with breads, cheeses, fruits, and meats.

"How is yer training at Urquart going son?" Stefan asked.

"Good Da, tis mainly paperwork though."

"How is Kenneth?"

"He's well, tires very quickly when things grow boring, tis easy enough though."

"Aye I ken tha, ye ave te fight te stay awake in those tedious, petty quarrels they ave."

"Dolan, how are ye brother? Are ye married yet?" Elford teased his brother.

"I'm good thanks Elf! Nae wed yet." He replied, grinning.

"Ave ye sin them bonnie red heads at the Forge Dolan?"

"Oh, here we go again, men, one track mind!" Meredith chirped in.

"Aye, I've met Harriet, she's nice but I've nae met er sister Maisie yet."

"Harriet's quite sweet on ye I reckon Dolan." Stefan added.

Dolan just shrugged his shoulders as they all continued to chat. The Maids were all busying themselves around them and prepping the bed chambers upstairs. Kitchen cooks were readying the meats for the supper feast, Beef, Pheasant, and Mutton.

"Reet well it as bin a long ride Father, Mother, I'm gonna head up fer a nap, freshen mi clothes n' soak in a tub if ye dinnae mind?"

"Aye son, I think we can manage te let ye go fer a while." Stefan and Meredith smiled.

Elford rose to go upstairs but not before whispering to his father.

"Will ye invite Angus n' his daughters te the feast tonight, Father?"

"Aye son, be mi pleasure." Stefan grinned as he met his wife's eyes.

"Where does he get his wild side from love?" She asked.

"I dinnae ken wifey, nae me!"

Dolan looked on, seemingly a little put out that his younger twin brother was hogging all the limelight at the moment, but he knew better and remained silent.

Later that evening the feast was held and whilst everyone sat eating and drinking, Pipers from Boreraig started to play outside the hall. Since the settlement there had gone up, a few of the men had been coming down to Dunvegan once a week to teach folks here, it sounded amazing.

The tables and benches had all been pushed back against the walls as Stefan and Meredith led the dancing. When the floor began to fill with other couples, they went and sat back down on the dais. Elford rose from his seat.

"Wish me luck Father!" He walked across the room to the MacDerum family.

"Ma'am, may I have this dance?" Elford bowed and offered his arm to Maisie.

Maisie looked at her father, he nodded. She quickly turned back to Elford with a big smile on her face and allowed him to escort her to the floor. Elford placed a hand at her waist and held the other in the air as she took his hand and laid the other on his chest. There gazes met and held. Laird Stefan and Lady Meredith watched, a little stunned by his brazen efforts that seemed second nature to him. Although Stefan was pleased that he was braw enough and didn't require any assistance, Meredith was more concerned that he conducted himself properly as a gentleman, in the lady's presence. Dolan sat and watched his brother too; he is the eldest, but Elford always seemed more at ease when around ladies. Dolan thought ladies were nice to have as friends, but he wouldn't cause a fuss about one.

"Sir Dolan, may I have this dance please?"

It was Harriet MacDerum! She stood in front of the dais with her hand held out, looking quite nervous.

"Oh, of course he will dear! Come on, get up Dolan, the lady awaits." Meredith gave him a gentle push and Stefan smiled.

Dolan and Elford took the floor several times throughout the evening as they spun around, weaved, and danced with their newest lady friends. Their parents sat, holding hands under the table, watching their sons, watching everybody having a grand time of things. Angus was also watching the frivolities closely.

Caitlin Mary, the Laird's youngest and now twelve summers old was dancing with Colby. She looked lovely, a smaller version of her mother. One day men would fight over her hand thats for sure, but hopefully that would be a few years away yet.

It was getting quite late now, and the Laird and his wife bowed and left for their chambers. Angus left with his daughters too. It wouldn't be too long before the entire hall and everything quietened for the night.

Stefan stood at the window in his chamber, stretching his muscled arms out. The sun is rising early today, and he wanted to get on. As he peered out of the window at Loch Dunvegan, he noticed how still the waters looked, the lands were peaceful and stunning to the eye. He spotted two figures walking along the shoreline towards the gardens below the castle, he squinted his eyes and realised it was Elford and Maisie who were taking a walk, unchaperoned! He wondered if her father knew she was out, alone with his son but it wasn't his business, he had to let the boys live their own lives. He was once that young and it wasn't easy to find ladies as beautiful as these two red heads. Harriet was brave to step forward and ask Dolan to dance and Stefan admired that in a woman as long as they did it with flair.

In the main hall Dolan was already seated breaking his fast when Stefan and Meredith approached. Sat opposite Dolan was Harriet, with her head bowed.

"Good morning to ye both, we assume ye enjoyed last night's event?" Stefan asked.

"Oh yes My Laird, very much, thank ye kindly." Harriet responded.

"Aye father, we did."

Throughout the day Dolan and Elford were seen showing their new lady friends around the castle, folks nodded and waved, some spoke kindly to them and made them all feel very welcome. The ladies were becoming quite popular, and they asked questions about old oil paintings that hung around the castle's inner walls, the long tapestries and heirlooms with ornate carvings on. The twins were both men now, they needed space so they could live their own lives, just as Stefan and Meredith did when they were the same age.

Meredith hadn't been sleeping very well lately, it seemed to take her hours to drop off, only when she finally did, it was usually almost dawn and time to rise anyway! The short sleeps she did manage to get began to worry her and she dreamed of witches, old ruins and her sons.

Nicholas had told his wife Isla, to visit the Healer. She's constantly weak and has vomited for quite some time now. They were wed several years ago, and Stefan had given them a chamber within the castle. Maids had commented on her lessening appetite and how pale faced she looked, so she agreed to go and speak with the Healer. Isla is only just five foot tall and of a very slight build, everything about her is dainty in appearance. When she spoke to Gwen, she had asked her when her last monthly flow was.

"Three or four months ago Isla?

"Nae Gwen, tis nigh on a year noo." Isla replied.

"Come, get yourself laid on this table and I will examine your stomach. Thats it. My dear, you are with child! Your womb feels very full, although you are quite slim but definitely full here. I'd estimate about seven months on."

Isla fainted! Good job she was laid on the table. After about ten minutes Isla came too and promptly threw up all over Gwen's feet!

"Oh nae, I'm so sorry Gwen."

"Never mind that Isla, it's normal, have a sip of water and rest easy for a few minutes, I will just see my next patient and return to you."

Ten minutes later, Gwen walked back into the room, followed by Nicholas, Isla's husband.

"I'll give you two a few minutes together, then I will return, alright Isla?" She nodded.

"Love, why did ye faint? Are ye alreet?"

"Aye I think so, but Gwen said sumet te me."

"Sumet tha made ye faint? Wha did she say?"

"She said I am between seven and eight months with child!"

Suddenly Nicholas felt dizzy, and he reached out for the edge of the table. Isla saw the look in his eyes and called for Gwen. She came running in and held his arms, pushing him back in the chair at the same time.

"Here drink this, slowly now, deep breaths."

"Love, did ye say ye were with child?" He asked.

"Aye thas reet n' it'll nae be long before the bairn is wi us either."

"The reason I called ye husband Isla, is because you fainted just as he almost has done too. You are very slim and set with thin bones, you have already been sick and weak for a while noo. I'm a little concerned that you may not have enough strength in your body right now for you and the bairn, so we must make a plan and stick to it. I think you need special food measures for you both, the bairn needs to be healthy to be born and you need to be stronger to go through the birthing process Isla."

The seriousness was obvious within Gwen's voice. She was quite concerned. Nicholas will have to watch her closely and ensure she takes food and water in every hour and try to put on a little weight. Nicholas commented that he'd have a quiet word with Colby to see if he could lessen his work hours just for a few weeks, maybe take lighter duties to allow regular visits back to see Isla.

Mortal Harmony

The Dunvegan and Urquart elite teams continue to scour the lands for any trouble or hot spots of unknown activity. They only move at night and remain hidden during the day. So far, they have avoided all trouble, things have been relatively quiet across the Highlands. Their task was to only observe, attack only if attacked. Several hot spots had been added to the one and only map which Stefan had, he'd kept it safe and very secure. Every few weeks one man would return and report to base, updating the Laird of any happenings, he'd stay for five days then return to his group, then another man would set off and ride for home.

The Maids were cleaning their Laird and Lady's chamber, dusting and refreshing the linen sheets, as they worked, they chatted quietly.

"Did they ever find the baby rattle Lady Meredith lost?"

"Nae, I dinnae think so."

"Reet, well we'll keep an eye oot fer it, I ken it meant a lot te er."

It was obvious they were talking about the baby rattle that Meredith seemed to have mislaid. All her three children had used it when they were bairns, and it was quite a sentimental item. Meredith really wanted to keep it safe, but it had vanished, then it appeared a few years back hanging from the belt of a ghostly Piper at Glenfinnan, never to be seen again!

Nicholas had now had a talk with Colby regarding his concerns for Isla, he'd agreed to allow him the necessary time off without a problem. Colby had lost a bairn too when Tina was badly rat bitten and ended up in a sever fever. They'd been trying for a bairn for years, but nothing seemed to happen. Now all they seem to do is argue because she wants to age with Colby. Tina doesn't want to be forever young and lose everyone, everything she knows here.

Unbeknown to Colby, Tina had visited the Fairy Pools on Skye. Stories say that wherever Danu bathed, she left a small amount of energy, power in some cases, unless she took it away. Tina being Seelie Fae, knows it's also a portal of sort and she is able to send messages to Danu who finds a way of responding but not verbally. You never see her; she just finds way of letting you know her response. The message Tina sent stated she wanted to be mortal and age with her husband. Now all she had to do, is wait for an answer.

Lady Meredith had taken a walk through the village and

past the market stalls. She was pleased to see the farmer who had fully restocked all his Eider Ducks, as he lost them all to the Ergotism a while ago. Everything looked plenty healthy as they waddled about quacking around their little pond. It had a small central island on with a little wooden house and a ramp leading to door holes, just big enough for the ducks to enter in. It was a real pleasure to watch them, and it made her feel happy.

"Hello Father Beeforth, how are you?" Meredith asked as she passed him.

"My Lady, I am fine thanking ye, mi old bones are playing up a little. Och, ye should visit the chapel whilst yer oot, go n' see mi replacement. He seems rather nice; I'll be happy when I can retire."

"Oh Father Beeforth, surely it's just the cold thats been affecting your bones, the weather will warm soon, it'll help."

"Nae I dinnae think so My Lady. Anyhow, his name is Father William O'Brian, like Helga's, he wor from an orphanage, then he took up the cloth in Ireland."

"Oh, I will pop in and say hello, but you must take care now."

Meredith continued her walk through the village. She never asked for a guard to accompany her, but Stefan always ensured a few followed her at a discreet distance. Of course, she was aware, but didn't mind, it gave her a feeling of security.

It was a warm spring morning and life around the market stalls appeared quite lively. Plenty of folk busied themselves, either selling or buying goods when two familiar faces came into view.

"Hello you two! Having fun? Oh! Dolan with Harriet too, eh? How are you dears, I hope they are treating you well ladies?" Meredith asked.

Both the boys and their lady friends were walking through the village and the market quite openly, everybody could see them. It would spark a few gossipers off no doubt, but the young men were proud to show the beauties on their arms.

"Shall you all be having supper with us tonight? Meredith asked.

"Aye Mother, will all be theer, see you later." Elford replied.

Things seemed to be getting quite serious with the twins and their lady friends, the courting couples as Stefan would say, Meredith smiled and wondered if there would be any weddings soon. Maybe two!

"Anna, please can we have some Bannocks to take down to Father Beeforth and some for Father O' Brian too, can you ask a Maid to take them? Oh, you're not Anna?" Meredith was surprised by the strange face in front of her.

"My Lady hello. I am also named Anna; I have just taken over the other Anna's duties as she wishes te retire."

"Oh, I see, so you were promoted from within?"

"Aye My Lady, I think the other Anna wants te tek up sewing again n' reading. She's sits wi Lady Mary as she sleeps, sometimes she reads te er tae."

"Thats worked out quite well for her then, she's known Mary all her life."

"Yes, My Lady, well I must crack on n' yes, I will see te the bannocks tae Ma'am."

"That will be grand, thank you." Meredith left the kitchens.

She was tired now; the exercise and the fresh air had done her good and she was pleased the boys were both happy. Maybe she'd just lay on the bed, with the window open and the gentle breeze blowing over her face, it would help her take a nap. But as she fell asleep, her dreams began. Back to Dunscaith Castle ruins, the witches and her sons. She woke up screaming her lungs out with Stefan holding her arms, calling her name!

"Och love, yer wor screaming very loud, it dinnae half scare me, are ye alreet?"

"Yes, I think so. A little tired."

"Wor ye back at Dunscaith?" Meredith nodded.

"I'm gonna ave te call ye Scathach if ye dinnae stop soon

"No, I cannae hide. I'll go n' tell Colby noo, he's a good man, he'll understand." She thought.

She found Colby in the rear training yards.

"Och love! I ken it meant a lot te ye but I dinnae wan ye te die, ever."

"I dinnae wanna be alone, ever either. I want us te be tagitha." Tina replied to Colby.

"I ken love. We'll hold each other up then, in our final days, side by side."

They hugged. Warmth, understanding and love prevailed. Two mortals in harmony.

No Weeping

At breakfast everyone sat down eating porridge, some had eggs and freshly baked bread, others chose to just eat bannocks. Stefan and Colby were in mid conversation when they heard the village bells toll. The pattern meant Caution to All!

Men on the battlements called down, a mass body of people were approaching! Men, women, children, some animals too! In fact, it was almost everyone from Urquart Castle! They looked tired and battered for some unknown reason.

"Wha the ells gannin on?" Stefan yelled.

"Colby, open the gates, let them in, stay alert men. Someone let Anna ken to get cooking more food n' drinks tae. Boys, get more logs te the chambers, light the fires all round, fetch blankets te the hall, step te it men!"

Elford watched as his own villagers and several guards asked him to go to the study for a briefing of events. Stefan, Colby, and Dolan led the group in haste.

"Sir a lot as happened since ye left Urquart fer ere." A beaten-up guard was trying to relay the occurrences.

"Sit doon Seamus, take a breath." Stefan poured the man a whisky.

"There ye go, get tha doon ye throat. Noo, tell us what exactly appened at Urquart?"

"Sir, Laird Kenneth passed in his sleep, peacefully it seemed. We were all in the study aving a meeting as te whar we dae next, n' who would be Laird. It wor looking like most men wanted fer Elford ere, te stand his new seat, but the call of attack went up and stopped everything! Our seven elite team must ave seen em coming in the gates and they rushed back te elp. They fought the creatures bravely, our guards tae! But they wor all slaughtered Sir! Everyone o' em, cut doon like meat, blood everywhere, it wor bad." Seamus held his head in his hands, tears were running down his face in sadness of all the death and destruction he'd witnessed.

"Only a few o' our guards left n' led the village folk te safety out the back te the forest, then te the ferry where many boats and birlinns waited us. They'd heard the ruckus n' thank the lord had waited fer us. If they'd left, we would surely ave all perished. Many folk had already lost their lives, some o' the bairns have been hurt tae, mainly from been trampled on in the rush. The boats brought us all ere te Skye, where we came te you asking fer shelter My Laird. May we stay?" Seamus looked up at Stefan, his eyes pleading for help.

"Aye, ye can all stay, nae worries theer. Open the doors, bring everyone indoors, eat, drink n' get warm. Tell your village folk. Colby sort the Healers te come straight away please."

The inner doors flew open, and several Maids rushed in bring platters of food, drinks and extra blankets, chairs were spread out and fires were roaring heat around. Empty chambers upstairs had been allocated to the larger families with young children, they were shown to their new rooms to rest. Food would be brought up to them with milk for the children.

Stefan is furious but very saddened to hear of Laird Urquart's passing, he liked Kenneth and considered him a good friend. He also knew this would be a test for Elford and worried a little although he'd offer his full support and stand behind him. Dolan had realised what this meant. A war had been started!

"Colby can ye sift te Helga's, ask er fer advice please, aboot these creatures we dinnae ken?"

"My Laird, on it noo." He replied.

"Hello laddie, come on in!" Helga said smiling.

"Always a pleasure Ma'am."

"Noo then lad, sit doon, what can I dae fer ye on this fine day?"

Colby informed Helga of everything he had just heard in the study, her face wrinkled and winced at the loss of life. She always bore a sound opinion and her advice has aided their quests for many years now. Colby had hope in his eyes as he sat and tasted her summer berry wine.

"Colby, yer ken every dark creature, be it a whole army or an individual, but everyone one o' em as a weakness?"

"Aye."

"Well just like the battle a few years back, when the water wave, simply washed over the creatures n' dinnae effect em. It did result in flooding out all the rats' lairs, n' they ran te the dark masses who jumped inte the ocean, only te be devoured by Selkies? Can ye see what I'm saying Laddie?" Helga asked.

"Aye Helga, but..."

"Dinnae interrupt Laddie, ye asked mi fer mi opinion. I'll give it. Then yer can ask yer questions." She continued.

"The dark creatures hated the rats n' jumped te their deaths. Every action has a consequence. They are more or less opposites Laddie, just as actions n' consequences are. If ye can sort the

balance, ye can defeat em! Ye said the creatures are small, white furries in their many?"

"Aye Helga."

"Sounds like those from where I hailed at the Hill of Tara in Ireland. They can transform inte a huge dark mass wi sabre like teeth that'll scratch yer eyes oot before it kills ye."

Colby held his cup up to ask politely for another drink. Helga topped it up before he opened his mouth!

"Colby lad, the light from yer shields n' armour helped ye te defeat the dark creatures at the battle o' Fingal's Cave, small white n' fury, hmm. Mayhap their opposite, will help ye te defeat these? So sumet big, heavy, broad, loud, colossal tha kind o' thing. Dae ye see?"

"Bagpipes are very noisy, very loud. Folk singing n' banging drums can be loud tae Helga!"

"Aye ye could be reet, also the forests are full o' Pipistrelles lad, they are vera high pitched, so high we can barely hear them, but they deafen the dark creatures!"

"What are they?"

"Bats laddie, bats. Ye'd need te flush oot the bats te mek em screech so loud though."

"So how can we get the dark creatures te come te us?"

"Ye need to draw em oot lad, bait them, lure them oot.

"Dead animals, rotting fish anything wi a vile smell, mek a reet stench, it'll work I reckon."

"So, where dae ye think tis best te lure em tae Helga?"

"Thas easy. Where ye left off Laddie. At Glenfinnan."

"I could create a wave n' wash most out te sea tae!" Added Aria who sat patiently listening.

"Aye n' if the suns shining, we can try blinding em again tae. Tioram is hidden from the ocean, we could try the bait on theer. The Loch also has two mountains, one either side so any pipers or singers' voices shall echo n' travel doon the Loch."

"Mayhap tis wise te ask Ghilly te summon the Selkies again, they could stay in the ocean just off Tioram te catch any that escape. If the feedings good, I'm sure they'll swim up the Loch te greet em." Helga said.

"Sounds like a plan. Thank ye Helga. Kaylee, we must report back te the Laird, give yer friend a hug n' we'll be off lass." Colby bowed his head to Helga in respect.

"Bye Aria, Helga, we'll probably see ye soon at Glenfinnan then? Have care." Kaylee smiled at her friend, missing the days gone by when they shared a house together.

"Aye lass, I'm sure we'll both be theer te elp ye. I'll mention it te Nessy tae n' get er te keep an eye oot in the area."

"Thank ye again Helga."

Colby and Kaylee quickly dipped their toes into the edge of the Loch Ness's waters and quietly thanked Nessy for safe passage by. The tradition continued.

Back at Dunvegan, Stefan shook hands with Colby, glad to see his brother safely returned. He quickly called a meeting and Colby informed him of what Helga had discussed, along with help from Aria, Kaylee and Ghilly. Whilst Stefan thought it was a strange plan, it was evident that it was the only plan available, and he agreed. The meeting was interrupted by a knock at the study door. It was his seven elite team who had heard of the attack on Dunvegan and returned to help.

"My Laird good te see ye well, how may we help?"

"Tis good te see ye all safe n' well tae men, come in, sit doon. Thank ye fer ye service, it means a lot te us all ere. We live in dangerous times, but we must stick tagitha. It's what meks us stronger. We shall ave our revenge n' we shall slaughter this dark army tha threatens te tek our homes, our wives, our bairns n' our lands. Are ye with me men?"

The ayes went around the room and everybody cheered, they'd stand with Stefan and run into battle alongside him. The response was unanimous. It was war!

Whisky was passed around and everybody had a wee dram.

"Elite team, I want ye te stay ere n' guard our home with the women n' bairns in. I cannae leave ere wi out kenning our homes n' families are safe, alreet?

"Aye My Laird we ken, nae botha."

The details of the plans were discussed, and it resulted in Ghilly, Kaylee and Aria sifting a hundred men between them, to Glenfinnan. Other guards will split up and flank the sides of Loch Shiel but remain hidden until Stefan gives the call. Another group shall ride quietly towards Tioram, there they'd dismount, leaving the horses hidden in the nearest treeline and walk to Tioram ruins to set the bait. Sacks of straw would be positioned just in the front of the ruins, so it could be visible from Glenfinnan as much as possible. They'd have a few days to do this before the main group of guards arrived at the head of the loch armed with bagpipes and drums.

Dolan and Elford would be riding alongside their father, Urquod would be riding alongside his Sire too. Dolan would lead one flanked group of men and Elford the other side flanked group. Laird Stefan would stand at the head of Glenfinnan on the huge boulder, where in the past a Fae Prince once stood with Lady Meredith, whilst she was half naked. He remembered that day and it made him shudder to think of it, even now.

When Ghilly's group landed, he walked toward the water and held his arms up in front of his chest and mumbled something. He'd summoned the Selkies and sent word about an impending battle within two days' time. There would be food for them if they worked to help him. Helga had already sent word to Nessy, she had brought the Dolphins from the Moray Firth with her too. The ocean was full of hidden creatures, yet nobody would have suspected, there was nothing to see on its surface, as yet!

As dawn approached, Meredith had woken and put her feet on the floor at her bedside. When she stepped onto something cold, hard and flat! It was a Blacksmith's file, and she had no idea how it had got there. Nobody else knew as she asked the Maids.

Laird Stefan, Elford and Dolan stood in Castle Dunvegan's main hall, facing the men, and awaiting his word. Their lady friends Harriet and Maisie stood outside with all the other wives and children. They held onto each other obviously feeling very worried as to what was to come. Meredith recognized their jitters; she walked over and hugged them both.

"Now, now ladies, no weeping. We have to be strong, stick together, don't let the men see you worrying like this. Lift your chins, smile, and nod, be proud of your men ladies."

The young women gave a false kind of smile, but it was an improvement on the tears. Meredith remembered Anna's words, the old cook. She'd retired now and spent most of her days sat sewing at Mary's bedside whilst she had her long sleep. Sometimes Anna would soak a small piece of clean linen into a wine glass and let it drip gently onto Mary's lips. Anna swore she'd seen Mary lick it off with her tongue, but she remained asleep. Anna had comforted Meredith when Stefan took off and rode into battle when she was younger, she knew the feelings they all felt.

"I love you hubby." Meredith said to Stefan as he mounted the Black.

"Nae as much as I dae ye love." He squeezed her hand in reassurance.

"Ave care Mered's, we shall return in a few days." He

nodded a bow and she understood.

Scathach Rides Again

The bait worked! A dark mass appeared near Tioram. It hovered just above the cold waters of Loch Shiel, and it grew thicker and wider. Small furry creatures sprang out of it, only a few but they landed on the rocky shore of the ruined Tioram Castle. Stefan nodded to his Archers who immediately let loose a volley of fire arrows that directly hit the straw sacks the men had left a few days prior. It set the island a blaze and made a memorable landscape of silhouette ruins. One that would stick with them for some time. The fire and smoke had awakened the Bats, they began flapping and screeching around, the black mass began to show hundreds of pairs of sabre like teeth, all pointing towards Glenfinnan, where the arrows came from. The Bat colony took flight and circled above the ruins, darting in and out the thick smoke, their screeching even louder now. It sent the black mass into a fury, and it advanced towards the head of the Loch. Some of the creatures were swimming at the water's edge, others seemed to be crawling over the rocky shores, but they all went in one direction, Glenfinnan.

"Hold men, hold. Wait fer mi order!" Stefan called to his men assertively.

"What the ell is tha? Hold men!"

Up the side of the Loch, riders approached. There were six riders in the group, which was being led by a woman! It was Lady Meredith along with five of Stefan's elite team. She wore a strappy leather outfit with a skirt fashioned as a Warrior Woman! Her long dark curls were trailing out behind as she galloped towards Stefan. Meredith looked wild, like Scathach herself!

The elite were carrying sacks filled with something. Stefan was horrified to see his wife like this and at such a time as a battle is about to commence. Then he became amazed at her bravery, stupidity but brave. Then he was turned on! The sacks were full of iron filings.

"Hello husband, trust me, Stefan!" She yelled over.

"Hurry men, quickly spread it out!"

The team opened the sacks and spread it out along the shoreline at the head of the Loch.

"Aria, your wave lass, hurry!"

Aria held out her arms above the Loch to chest height and began to mumble. A wave grew in height to the level of her arms, it picked up the iron filings as it swirled over and over. Aria then flung her arms towards to ocean end of the Loch, the wave gathered speed, height, and momentum. Helga called out to her.

"Again lassie, another!"

Aria repeated the process and sent many of the dark

creatures' way down the Loch to the open waters. That was the invitation needed for the Selkies who were waiting patiently out at sea. They swam at the Loch entrance near Tioram, biting and squeezing the life out of the dark creatures that had been carried along within the waves.

Meanwhile at Glenfinnan, only half of the creatures had been pushed back, others still approached. Stefan gave the order, his arm held high in the air and the Pipers began to play. The drums began to boom loudly, and men began to sing their hearts out. It was a truly magnificent sound that travelled along the deep mountain sides, all the way to the sea. The men warmed as they hollered out their tunes, the Pipers could be heard for miles around the Highlands. It was also deafening to the dark creatures!

A battle took place out at sea, under the water in the Loch and along the shoreline. Nessy had joined the ranks, according to Helga, the Unseelie were her favourite food. She couldn't be seen but Helga knew she was there! Nessy had also brought with her more Dolphins from the Moray Firth and the Cirein Croin! It's a massive sea serpent, once said to have devoured seven whales in one mouthful! Loch Shiel's waters turned black, as the creatures perished and turned to ash. Others were devoured never to be seen again. Men continued to sing aloud, Pipers played their hearts out, the drums boomed and struck their own echoes. They all stood and watched as the final group of dark Unseelie seen in the distance

Laird Stefan kissed his wife and lingered on her lips.

"Come on, let's go home Scathach! Meredith smiled as all the groups gathered and began the long journey back to Dunvegan.

Dunvegan village bells tolled. Its pattern meant the Laird returns.

Village folk from Dunvegan and Urquart came rushing out to greet them. Children, women, other guards, and elderly folk, all stood waving as they passed by.

"Well done My Laird." A woman called out to Stefan who nodded in response.

Harriet and Maisie stood patiently at the gates. Their stomachs all knotted up, their nerves churning. Stefan dismounted first, handing the Black to the stable boys. He went to help Meredith down and let his hands loiter around her waist as her feet hit the floor.

"I'll deal wi ye, laters!" He grinned.

Elford and Dolan dismounted, to be met by their lady friends who slammed into their chests, tears falling heavily down their cheeks. Stefan and Meredith stood holding hands, watching their sons embracing their ladies with passionate kisses!

"Awe thats beautiful Stefan." Meredith said.

'Och tis doon reet filth tha!" He grinned at her again.

Food and drinks awaited everyone in the main hall. Anna

the new cook had done them proud, and Meredith adored her scones with fresh cream.

On the way home Mary had told Stefan, she had woken up in the Tween Realm and assumed she had died. But then she had found a glass bowl, the bowl had tiny green gems set around the sides and seemed to be full of wine! Well, as she didn't like waste, she drank it! The next thing she knew she came to on her bottom near Tioram and Elford was picking her up!

Anna the old cook who had retired, had been sat in a chair in Mary's chamber reading quietly to her. She'd fallen asleep herself, not realising Mary's body had vanished from the bed and didn't wake up until the village bells tolled.

Ghilly had been furious that children had been hurt by the dark Unseelie creatures at Urquart, he loved children, especially those in need of help. Many had severe bruises on their tiny bodies, others were scratched and bumped, but all were alive and recovering at Dunvegan now. As everybody else had travelled back home, he had sifted to Urquart and summoned all his forest friends, the Seelie men who came to his call for help. They were dwarves too and wore all green shades of clothing, they all had beards, and several were smoking pipes filled with dried leaves.

The Seelie men and Ghilly erected a large tent in the field outside the castle, where food and drinks were made available to all. Plus, a place for shelter as they worked. Although these men were ale lovers so Ghilly made it clear, the drinks to be kept light until the work was completed and they could have more as a reward. That made these little guys quite merry.

There was a lot of work to be done and their aim firstly, was to rebuild the thatch roofs on the villagers' homes. Once that was done, they'd look at the castle although any blockwork would need to be done by others, the work there been too heavy for these little guys. There was a lot of other items to be cleared up before all of that commenced too.

One hundred and fifty forest fellows helped Ghilly, and they seemed to be working in small groups of six, which proved to be effective, their jobs were being completed quite quickly. The fellows also gathered up sheep and cattle that had drifted away from the initial ruckus into the forests. Putting them into enclosures and repairing the fences, but the farmers themselves would need to sort out who's was who's when they returned. During that time, Ghilly had quickly sifted back and spoke with Stefan. He needed about a week to get things to an acceptable level for folk returning and Stefan had agreed. He'd also talk to Elford about it, and they'd discuss what would happen from there. Stefan had already vowed to help Elford to rebuild Urquart even better and stronger than before.

What was left of Urquart people, the guards and the council

of advisers had all agreed for Elford to take the Laird's seat. He'd gladly accepted, but an official ceremony with pledges of allegiance would take place at a later date.

"Colby, dae ye ave a few minutes spare?" Elford asked.

"Aye lad, are ye alreet?"

"I want yer opinion if yer please?"

"Alreet lad, I'll try, go on."

"Marriage. When dae ye ken tis the reet time n' choice?"

"Whoa, thas a big step lad! If yer truly love a lassie, n' she feels the same, ye'll ken when n' what the right choice is yer sen."

"Aye well, we both want it, Colby."

"Are ye sure tis love lad, nae lust?"

"Och yeah, we ken all aboot tha tae!"

"Well, I dinna see a problem then! But ye must speak wi yer Da, lad."

"Aye I will but dae ye think he'll accept two?"

"Two what? Two women?" Colby raised his brow.

"Nae, two marriages, in one ceremony?" Elford chuckled at Colby's reaction.

"Oh, who, eh?"

"Och Colby, ye are daft sometimes, Dolan n' I, te wed Harriet n' Maisie."

"Och bloody ell! Thas a shock but aye, it meks sense I suppose. As long as thas what ye all want, go n' speak te yer Da lad?"

"Aye, I'll go noo, cheers Colby."

Dolan and Elford took a deep breath as they stood outside their father's study door. They gently knocked. No answer. They knocked a little louder and the door opened.

"Hello boys, come in." Meredith answered.

"Dolan, Elford, are ye alreet lads?" Stefan said.

"Aye Father, we'd like a word please."

"Oh, man to man talk! I'll leave you to it then." Meredith said.

"Nae Mother, we would like ye te hear. Stay please."

Elford appeared to be doing all the talking and as Meredith sat down, she wondered if one of their lady friends was with child, she silently betted herself it was Elford, due to Dolan's quietness.

"Father, Mother, we wish te wed!"

Stefan sat at his desk, a whisky in hand, his mouth open, a little shocked!

"Nae tagitha, te Maisie n' Harriet, but at the same time.

"Oh, a double wedding!" Meredith squealed excitedly.

Neither of the twins got a chance to answer their mother, for she had jumped up from her chair and grabbed them both in a bear hug!

"Oh my, this is going to be a huge celebration boys. I'm so proud of you both."

There wasn't an inch of un-kissed skin left on their cheeks!

"Sons, I'm proud of ye both tae, ye ave our blessing." Stefan moved in for a family hug.

"Lads ye ken, any heirs ye produce will be vera important bairns, that'll need protection at all times?"

"Aye Father, but we ain't got te the bed chambers yet, gis a chance Da!" Elford responded.

"Oh, ye must ask Caitlin to be your bridesmaid." Meredith added.

They were interrupted by another knocking at the door!

"Och Colby, come in, ave ye heard the good news?" Stefan asked smiling.

"The twins are getting married Colby!"

"Och lads, I'm proud of ye, well done. If ye need any womanly advice, come te me, ye father, nae ken it all!" Colby smirked.

"I assure you Colby, he's a master!" Meredith butted in.

"I ken I'm only ere te bloody pay fer the stuff ye all spend!" He laughed along with them.

"Anyway, My Laird. I ave some news of mi own." Colby announced.

"Aye, go on." Stefan was intrigued.

"Ye ken our Tina became mortal, when she gave up ere Fae abilities?"

"Aye."

"She's noo with child! I'm gonna be a Da!" Colby beamed from ear to ear.

"Och Colby, thas brilliant news, well done ye. Mayhap the lads, ought te see ye fer advice then!" Stefan smiled.

"I'm so pleased for the both of you." Meredith added as Dolan and Elford shook his hand.

"Reet, I reckon we'll call a feast tonight te mek these announcements then eh? Say one weeks' time lads?"

"Blimey, I'd better start planning!" Meredith said in a panic.

"Aye Father, a week, then I'll ride home wi mi new wife n' tek the Urquart seat as Laird."

"Dolan, after the wedding, ye n' Harriet are welcome te stay in a chamber here, together."

"Thank ye Father, I will speak te Harriet, but I must go n' speak wi ere Father noo."

"Aye son, Angus will be pleased fer ye both."

The week ran by in a blur. Everything happened really quickly as all plans fell into place nicely. Flowers were picked and huge swags were draped across the paintings and tapestries around the main hall and adjoining rooms. Tents were erected outside with tables and chairs. There would be a large ceremony with an outdoor garden feast as villagers from Urquart were sleeping in the halls, this way everybody could attend. The castle chapel shall be used for the joint ceremony, and it too was adorned with flags and garlands of flowers.

Cooks were busy cooking hog roasts and Maids were chopping vegetables, potatoes and prepping the puddings. A multitude of fresh fruits had been brought up from the Apple Orchard too, along with different types of berries which went along lovely with Anna's fresh cream scones.

Pipers from Boreraig were also heading down for the event. Seamstresses were busy sewing gowns for Caitlin, Mary, Harriet, Maisie, Isla, Tina, and Meredith. They all matched and were cream silks, decorated with tiny blue harebells, it will be lovely. Invitations had gone out, be it quickly and Aria and Helga will be coming too.

Whilst training at Urquart, Elford had learned of an old alliance with the clan Fraser, and he wished to reopen and strengthen it so he invited Laird Fraser and his wife to the wedding. The Laird had replied and agreed to attend along with a few of his guards naturally. They also sent their condolences for the passing of Laird Kenneth of Urquart. Elford had spoken to his father about this, and they'd agreed to hold a ceremony at some point, to mark the passing and honour Laird Kenneth. Then follow it up with his own Laird ship ceremony and the pledges.

The Healers, Gwen and Caroline had been up to speak with Stefan too. Gwen wished to remain at Dunvegan, whilst Caroline been a little younger, wanted a little more adventure still and wished to go to Urquart with them when they returned. Elford and Stefan had agreed this, it would be very helpful to restart with a Healer present. Gwen, it seemed, had developed a close friendship with Blacksmith Angus MacDerum and folk were watching it blossom.

Stefan called his seven-elite team into his study and informed the of a slight change to his plans. Three of the Dunvegan elite team would be based at Urquart. One man would continue the return run to relay messages, remain five days then regroup and rotate with another man. A run between Urquart and Dunvegan will now be carried out by the elite team so one man would always be on the move relaying messages. Their duties were the same, to remain hidden and map out any trouble or hot spots of activity. The seven of them agreed and took off that night. But as the elite team left the study, Helga knocked on the door. Colby stood behind her.

"Stefan, Laird, are ye theer?" Helga called.

"Aye Helga, come in, how are ye?"

Colby held out the chair as Helga sat down before seating himself against a rear wall. Stefan handed out a glass of whisky to each of them to which Helga downed it in one gulp and didn't even gasp! The men took a sip and savoured the taste, Stefan poured another dram for Helga.

"Laird, the battle on Loch Shiel, it wor only the start, we dinnae defeat em! Morrigan had just gone further oot te sea. A huge battle wi thousands more creatures took place tha we dinnae ken. Many of our Selkies perished, along wi lots o' Moray Firth Dolphins. Nessy fought really hard n' were badly injured, though she'll live. The Cirein Croin even took severe injuries due te the mass of creatures, there were thousands, many more than we thought at the time. What's left of our saviours ave noo gone inte hiding te heal. It'll be many years before we can get any elp from them again, if ever! Morrigan was eventually defeated, nae before she vowed her work would continue. We cannae stop em opening portals as they wish, but we did greatly reduce their numbers fer a time tha is! All we can hope fer in our lifetime noo, is tha there will nae be quite so many, other than the odd scout."

Stefan and Colby took a bigger swig of whisky.

"Och Helga, I dinnae ken any o tha oot at sea! I cannae imagine the damage tha thousands more o' them dark creatures could dae, thas terrible Helga." Stefan was shocked.

"Aye tis, well laddies, I've said all I needed te say noo, I'll be off home te Aria. Thanks, fer the drinks." Helga turned and left the study.

Stefan and Colby looked at each other, amazed at what they had just heard!

The Ceremonies

Dolan and Elford stood tall, smart, and masculine, at the head of the aisle in Dunvegan chapel, facing Father O'Brian. They certainly were a sight, standing side by side donning their clan tartan, in kilts with white linen shirts, swords at the hip and the emblem of a stag pined at their shoulders. Laird Stefan and Colby wore identical outfits, but Stefan had several pins as Laird. His sword bore a green gem upon the hilt. It matched the tiny gem within Meredith's wedding ring and the pendant she wore around her neck. Unbeknown to the boys, Stefan had the Blacksmith forge two more gems into the hilt of two new swords, he had made for them, specifically for this day. The green gems were from Tir Na Rog, Danu's Great Garden and are irreplaceable.

Lady Meredith wore a beautiful gown of pale blue silk, which had slits cut at the hips down to the lower hem, allowing their clan tartan to poke through and be seen to all. Her hair was plaited up into a top knot with long dark curls left dangling at the side. Harebells had been added to form a tiara look. She was stunning and felt good in herself.

Meredith had just left the brides. They were ready and

Angus was set to walk in between the down the aisle.

"Are ye ready Maisie love?" Angus proudly asked his daughter.

"Aye Father, I cannae wait."

"Are ye ready tae Harriet?"

"Nae Father, I cannae dae this." Harriet took off out of the chamber, down the corridor, the back stairs and out of site to everyone! She was gone!

"Och nae. Wor am I te tell Dolan?" Angus lowered his head.

"Let's gan on doon love, we'll get ye te ye groom, eh?"

When they reached the chapel door, they paused, and Angus beckoned a nod to Colby. Colby calmly rose and went to see him.

"Sir Harriet's gone, I dinnae ken where, she just ran off saying she cannae do this. I'm so sorry. Will ye tell Dolan n' see if Elford wishes te proceed, I ken everyone's waiting."

"Och nae, I'm sorry tae. I will tell Dolan noo."

Colby walked towards Dolan and whispered in his ear. Dolan turned to his parents, his eyes glazed in silence as he squeezed his mother's hand and walked directly out of the chapel doors. Eyes from the guards followed him, just as Maisie and Angus entered and began walking down the aisle. Angus stopped, placed a hand on Dolan's shoulder and lowered his eye lids. No words were needed. Dolan understood and hurried away from the gathering crowds. Meredith stood up to chase after him, but Stefan held her arm tightly and pulled her back into her seat.

"Nae Mereds, ye must leave them te sort it oot. Be ere fer Elford love."

She knew he was right, she nodded at her husband, lifted her chin, and smiled to support Elford and his wife to be. A musician began to play a Harp, temporarily diverting her thoughts but inside she was devastated for Dolan. She wondered how she could comfort him to make it feel easier. She diverted back when Stefan squeezed her hand and she saw the kissing couple in front of her. Cheers and whistles went up, the Pipers began to play outside, the villagers threw petals and rice over them as they walked down the aisle as man and wife, into the great outdoors to start their new life. The feasting commenced, but Meredith still felt devastated for her son.

"My Laird." Colby whispered quietly in Stefan's ear.

"Ye n' Meredith are wanted doon on the shoreline, if ye please, dinnae worry."

"Alreet Colby, we'll go noo."

Stefan and Meredith rose from their seats and left for the shoreline of Loch Dunvegan

"Mother, I'm sorry. Unlike her sister, Harriet does nae like crowds. She panicked n' ran. Here tis quiet n' Father O'Brian will wed us. Will ye bare witness fer us Da?"

"Oh son, we love you and Harriet. It was a bit daunting; we do have two castles full of folk here today too. We'll be glad te bare witness, won't we Stefan?"

"Aye of course we will." Stefan shook his hand and nodded, proud at his sons resolve.

Dolan and Harriet were married on the shores of Loch Dunvegan that evening as Stefan, Meredith, Colby, Tina and Angus watched. It was beautiful and thoughtful of Dolan, not to rush to any conclusions but to follow his heart and better the situation. It was intimate, lovely and Stefan knew then, his son would make a grand Laird in the future. He was ready.

"Will ye come back te the feast, both of ye?" Stefan asked.

Harriet nodded. She was still a little shy, but she adored Dolan, and he would support her to overcome her fears in time, according to her wishes and when she was ready.

Later in the study, Stefan gave his two sons their gift, the magnificent swords he had made for each of them. But he also wanted a quick chat with the twins.

"Lads, yer ken the small mark on the inner of ye wrists? Well on the morra, it will have changed n' it'll look like mine. Stefan showed his and although small in size it was definitely a clear image of an apple. The twins lifted their cuffs to compare just as Meredith walked in!

"Oh boys, what are you doing?"

"We were comparing Mother."

"I've heard that you men do that regularly, next time lock the door eh?" She giggled as the men burst out laughing.

"Mother, may we see ye ring please n' yer pendant?" Meredith held her hand up and wiggled her fingers, then pulled the pendant up from her chest.

"These are special green gems from Danu's Great Gardens of Tir Na Rog. We have some for Caitlin as she becomes of age too."

"Noo then lads, ye ave a duty te perform tonight, wha are ye doing still in ere? Get oot there wi yer new wives lads, mek em smile!" Stefan grinned as they left the study.

"Love do you think they'll be alright, will they manage?" Meredith asked Stefan.

"Aye love, they'll be fine. Once ye remove the stays, the laces come oot easily!"

"Oh, you, one track bloody mind! Right now, I'm hungry,

come on."

They left and returned to the feast, arm in arm, smiling and laughing at each other.

The next day a meeting was held in the main hall, even Laird and Lady Fraser attended as their guests. They watched and listened but remained quiet. Stefan had encouraged their alliance and had even put them up in a chamber whilst they visited for the ceremonies. Two guards stood outside their door as a mark of respect.

Elford took the floor and spoke clearly.

"This meeting is to discuss Urquart. We shall rebuild the castle and stand tall once again, better, stronger than ever. Are ye with me Urquart?"

Everyone shouted their ayes and banged on the tables in agreement. They had been treated well at Dunvegan. Given food, water, shelter and even treated for injuries by their Healer, but they really wanted to go home now.

It was decided. Tomorrow morning, they'd set off for the journey home. It would be a steady ride with wagons and cart loads of children and elderly folk, but they were prepared for it. Stefan had many horses, so a lot would ride, some chose to walk but would swap at certain points with riders who had saddle sores. Caroline had a cart of her own and it was full of Healing salves and potions to help get things set up at Urquart. She was grateful that

Gwen had helped her and had given her new bowls and blankets. They'd be fine and would see each other from time to time too.

Nicholas had been given charge of Dunvegan for a few weeks. His wife Isla had given birth to a baby girl not long past and as Nicholas took back up his duties, Stefan had given him use of a Maid to help Isla. It was Ideal for him to hold Dunvegan as he had done so previously, in the Laird's absence. This also allowed Meredith to attend Urquart with her husband.

The days passed, finally Elford rode up on Urquod and his wife on a grey mare as they approached the gates at castle Urquart. They had led the procession home followed by Stefan, Meredith, Dolan, Harriet, Colby, Tina, and many guards, plus all the village folk, the elderly, and the bairns.

Elford noticed several new flags were flying high above Urquart's turrets. Things looked as though they had been cleaned up. Houses in the village had been repaired, cattle and sheep were back in the enclosures, fences certainly had been repaired and the livestock had been given food and water.

At the gates, Ghilly stood waiting for them, Kaylee was behind him. Nearby, were Prudence, Janson and Hawk, a close-knit family if you'd ever seen one!

Everyone dismounted as villagers jumped down from their carts and walked to their homes. Several guards went with them, but everything was fine. Many repairs had been carried out.

"Welcome te yer new home Sir Elford." Ghilly stated as he past. Elford smiled back.

Stefan walked over to where Ghilly stood.

"Ghilly, where did ye put all the bodies? Especially the Lairds?"

"Outback Sir, in the field nearby. Tis neat n' tidy but we dinnae ken their names. The Lairds body we placed in the chapel tomb wi the rest of his clan. I hope thas alreet?"

"Aye Ghilly, well done."

Elford quickly assigned Maids, Cooks, Log Boys and Guards to various areas within the castle, and they immediately set to work. Other guards had erected a few more tents outside for sleeping, blankets and straw filled sacks were available to all. Inside the remainder of castle Urquart, the fires began roaring their warmth throughout the hallways. Some of the oil paintings and tapestries that hung in the great hall were badly damaged and scratched, but fortunately Aria's painting had survived, possibly because it was the only one to be locked inside the Laird's chamber at the time of the attack.

"Maisie love. Inside this door are our chambers, the Laird's room, n' nae one will enter without knocking n' being granted permission te dae so first." Elford told Maisie in an embrace.

He swung the door open and as they peeked through, they saw a huge four poster bed with fresh linens and bedside tables full of beautiful flowers. Elford bent down and swiftly picked up his new wife, carrying her across the threshold. He then did that man thing where they heel kick the door shut, Stefan used to do it and now Elford had learned the same thing! Elford walked them towards the bed, the drapes were open, and he gently laid his wife down with her head resting on the soft pillows.

"I love ye Maisie lass. I hope ye'll be happy ere, as mi wife!"

"Och ye soft sod, we'll be fine, come ere mi handsome man!" She held out her hand and beckoned him to join her on the bed, as their hug turned into a rather passionate kiss.

Suddenly the door burst open!

"Elford, do you want some supper? Oh, my lord! Oh, I'm so sorry!" Meredith walked in.

The kissing couple laughed but continued.

Later that evening, Meredith told Stefan what had happened as they got into their own bed at Urquart castle. Stefan laughed at her embarrassment.

"Dae ye remember being like tha yer sen, when we wor younger Mered's?" He asked.

"Yes, I do, but, well I suppose, I will have to get used to the fact that our sons have become men now."

"Anyway love, when we wor at Loch Shiel, where did ye find all tha gear tha ye wore?"

"You mean the leather strappy stuff?"

"Aye."

"Well, after I woke up with the file at my feet, I found the reason and just wanted to help with the iron filings. But as for the strappy gear, there was a chest sat in the corner of our room. I'd never seen it before and was curious to see what was inside. On the centre clasp I noticed a green gem, like ours."

"Aye, then what?" Stefan was eager to know.

"I opened it and put it on. It took a while as I didn't understand where all the various straps went on my body. There was a sword and a dagger too. Mayhap since I lost my inners, this has become my new purpose in life, the next chapter, eh?" She smiled.

"Did Danu put it there?"

"I dinnae ken who did laddie." Meredith mimicked his Scottish brogue again.

"Well te be honest love, when I first saw ye ride up wi yer hair blowing out long behind ye n' in all tha strappy stuff, in front o' mi men, I wor horrified! Then I found mi sen proud and amazed at yer bravery! Then I wor turned on! Thas my lassie theer. My wee gal! I'm loving this new purpose in yer life Mereds, come ere gggrrrrrr!"

The End.

The Laird and Lady MacLoud

Book 6

Please do leave a review on Amazon.

The Author

Barbara Raw

The Lairds & Lady MacLoud

Book 7
Caitlin Mary

by

Barbara Raw

Animal Instincts

Caitlin Mary MacLoud, daughter of Lady Meredith and Laird Stefan, Clan Chief of Castle Dunvegan on Skye, now eighteen summers old and an expert archer with equal horsemanship skills. Caitlin is a force to be reckoned with. Her beauty is very similar to her mothers, long deep brown curly hair, eyes the colour of the local burns and a character of strength and kindness with a high appreciation for nature.

Caitlin grew up aside two older brothers Dolan and Elford hence she's quite used to boisterous squabbles among men, although of late, the urges that young men seem to have, are raking on her nerves and she wishes for it all to stop! The only respite she gets is when she's mounted, galloping across the purple heathered moorlands with the wind blowing through her hair.

Caitlin's parents love her to bits and as a Laird's daughter, she's always been well protected, too much for her liking. She can fight and yield a sword as good as any man, if not better!

Caitlin craves adventure. Preferably where there are no guards trailing her every move. She just wants to be able to live, away from everyone's prying eyes.

Her parent's family lineage carry Fae blood within them,

somewhere on her mother's side. Lady Meredith used to sift about when she was carrying Caitlin as her unborn child. That fact ensured Caitlin carried undiscovered Fae abilities within her!

Laird and Lady Fraser, friends of her parents, are visiting Dunvegan castle with a couple of overnight stays.

Early one morning Lady Fraser stood and watched Caitlin as she worked with several different young horses. One was a yearling colt that was full of fizz. Her long curly hair was tied back in a leather thong, and she carried a short stick in her hand. When Caitlin arrived at the centre of the enclosed space, she unclipped the horse and let him loose to run about, to which he flew off kicking and bucking. A few guards had now gathered and were leaning on the fence watching her, intrigued as to what a woman could do that a man couldn't!

After a short while the youngster came to a standstill and just snorted, but it kept a careful watch on Caitlin. Then suddenly Caitlin took off running directly towards the horse, growling and hissing, scaring the life out of the colt and its flight instincts kicked in! The horse bolted off again as she continued to shoo it away from her. The horse shook its head in protest. Then Caitlin stopped and turned her back. Took three steps away, lowered her head to the ground and froze to the spot! The horse came to a standstill, puffing and snorting but slowly looked towards Caitlin to see what she was doing. He was intrigued and understood that he didn't need to run now.

Caitlin knew in nature, a herd would have their most important members on the inside of any group for protection, the mares and foals. The others on the outside would be guards or fighters. It works the same for Bees and many other animals.

The young horse calmed it's breathing and walked towards Caitlin in the centre. It nosed her sleeve and she calmly turned to face the horse whilst gently stroking his neck. Then she re-clipped him and led him back to his stall.

"Thats it fer tedae folks. Ye all ken noo, how he's joined up? He's learning his place, just keep the lessons short so he wants te work fer ye."

"Very impressive Caitlin." Lady Fraser said from over the fence.

"They learn their place within the ranks very early Lady Fraser, take Puppies or Pigs with multiple members. The fattest will always take the best teats and fight for their spot on the mother's belly. The weaker animals have the teats with the least amount of milk in."

"Amazing! How did you learn all this Caitlin?"

"Mainly by watching, studying, and reading books Ma'am. Did ye ken a sow carries her unborn piglets fer three months, three weeks, and three days? She lets er milk flow doon te the teat fer thirty seconds, every twenty minutes. Ye need te be a strong youngster te capture tha milk flow and grab the best teat! The point being rank is established early in the animal kingdom."

"Caitlin, will ye teach me? I'd love to learn all this n' how te ride as well. But I dinnae want any man teaching me. You could come n' stay wi us, at Fraser Castle, we can give ye a chamber of yer own n' even assign ye a Maid tae. On please say yes, it'll be lovely te have ye aroond!" Lady Fraser had crossed her hands.

"Oh er, actually it sounds quite tempting, tis a good offer, yes, I will come Lady Fraser."

"Fabulous, I can't wait. Will ye be ready te travel back wi us on the morra?"

"I will, thank ye."

Laird Stefan, Caitlin's father agreed as long as guards were present. Lady Meredith, her mother was really excited for her, as Caitlin had not really been away from the Dunvegan since she was born. It was about time she had an adventure for herself.

"Now Caitlin love, you will have the time of your life, trust me. Remember your sgian dubh at all times though and everything we ever taught you. But do have fun!" Meredith kissed her daughter as she waved her off.

Fifty guards from Dunvegan accompanied Laird and Lady Fraser's carriage, along with Caitlin on their journey home. Lady

Meredith ran up to the highest tower in Dunvegan castle, just to watch them disappear on the distant horizon. Tears began to flow. Laird Stefan finally caught up with her and came through the door puffing, his previously broken bones, although healed, sometimes played on his health.

"Och love, she's a woman noo, ye ave te let er go, let er live, as we ave done wi the lads. Tis difficult I ken, but Caitlin, well she'll be back, ye can count on it!" He hugged his sobbing wife.

The journey to Castle Fraser was delightful. There had been no trouble, the horses all behaved, and the weather turned out lovely. Half of the guards rode in front of the carriage and the other half rode at the rear. Caitlin wore her trews again, but she felt the men were watching her and talking about her. Not in a bad way, more of admiration of her riding skills. She sat deep and tall, proud in her saddle and the horse responded well to her ways. At one point Caitlin spun her horse around and rejoined the group at the rear.

"Lady Caitlin, I cannae allow ye te remain here fer ye safety." A fair headed man spoke.

"Fine, then just stay at my side, fer I ain't moving Sir!"

The guard did just that, all the way! He stayed at her side and never spoke a word! Caitlin watched him though; how he handled his horse and how big his thigh muscles were! Oh yes, she looked!

On arrival at Castle Fraser, Caitlin was met by a Maid who led her to her new chambers. They were stunning and she marvelled at huge oil paintings and tapestries from many years ago that had stood the test of time. The castle had, what must have been Scotland's largest tower house too! Her chamber looked out onto the gardens where she could see a large lake not too far away but even closer there was a small pond, full of beautiful dragon flies. She couldn't wait to get outside and explore the local wildlife when time allowed. The gardens were full of roses and their scent gently wafted up to her room on the breeze, awakening her senses. She was going to enjoy her time here.

A Maid came in with hot water and a tub for bathing, fresh linens for the bed and a tray full of fruit.

"Lady Caitlin, I'm Bella n' I'm vera pleased te meet ye. If ye need anything please, just ask."

"Thas vera kind of ye Bella, when we're in ere, if nobody else is aroond, dae call me Caitlin please."

"Thank ye Caitlin. Theres a wardrobe full o' clothes fer ye theer but I will ave te ask the seamstresses te mek sum more trews n' tunics fer ye."

"Nae mind, I've brought mi own. Would ye mind telling me

how te find the stables from ere? I'd like te see the horses."

Bella gave her the instructions; it wasn't the quickest route, but it would be the easiest for her until she found her way around.

Caitlin quickly bathed and thought she'd try to make a good impression, so she put on one of her few dresses. It was a deep green velvet type of fabric, long sleeved with a dipped front waist. The bodice was quite tight fitting with brown laces across the chest. She began to brush her hair out but left it long thinking it would dry quicker out in the sun. Her plans were to visit the stables, then the gardens before supper and maybe ride around the lake tomorrow.

Caitlin closed her chamber door, walked around the corner, and slammed straight into something rock hard! As her eyes focused on the darkened corridor, she realised it was the fair-haired guard, who she had ridden next to most of the way home!

"Och Lady Caitlin, are ye alreet?" He said in surprise.

"Oh my! I'm so sorry, I dinnae mean..."

"Nae it were my fault Lady Caitlin, I should ave bin more careful."

Caitlin nodded and continued her path, but not before recognising the smell his body gave off. It was sandalwood and jasmine, her Grandmother Mary makes that, and she loved it.

At the stables, two guards whistled at her, she turned to look but continued to walk down past the stalls. It was an impressive set up, she felt at ease among the aromas around the stables, the leather saddles, the hay and fresh straw, it was like being at home. Laird Fraser had some good-looking horses although these didn't appear to be quite as large as her father's. The Black was his huge War Horse, that had sired many of his mares and he was very proud of him.

Caitlin made her way back intending on locating the gardens, but as she neared the entrance where she came in, she heard a scuffle outside! Then another voice who was clearly shouting.

"Guards, tek them te the dungeons fer a night. I'll nae ave ye scrapping on mi watch!"

Caitlin walked past and spotted the fair-haired guard with a hard chest.

"The walled gardens?"

"Tha way Lady Caitlin, would ye...?" She'd gone!

He was going to offer his arm to lead her around the gardens safely, but she had scooted on past rather quickly.

"Eh gods, tha woman, stunning on the eye, kind in the heart n' the instincts o' a viper!"

He was quite taken with Caitlin and saw her character as a challenge. Let battle commence!

Horsemanship

"Are we starting training on the morra Caitlin?" Lady Fraser asked.

"Oh yes, at dawn then?" She replied.

"I'll be there." Lady Fraser smiled and nodded in excitement.

"Good morning, Lady Fraser."

"Oh, please Caitlin, call me Lillian."

"Of course, thank ye Lillian. Are ye ready?"

"Yes, where do we start?"

"Right at the bottom I'm afraid. I want ye te really ken a horse before owt else." Caitlin handed Lillian and fork, a shovel and a brush.

"Tadae we are mucking out the stalls, all o' these."

"Eh! Really?"

"Aye, tis the best way te learn n' ken what goes on Lillian. Dinnae fash, I'm ere te help ye."

It took them both most of the day to clear all of the stalls and it was hard work. They seemed to enjoy it though, chatting and giggling as they went along, it was good for them.

The following morning, Lillian could hardly walk down the stairs to break her fast, even lifting her arm to spoon her porridge into her mouth became a task and a half! Caitlin was stiff too but nowhere near as bad as Lillian. They both laughed over their food, today would bring a different chore which would use different muscles!

Caitlin handed Lillian a wooden carry tray with lots of different brushes and combs in.

"Start at the top and work down Lillian."

Once she had managed to lift her arms above her head, her muscles began to ease off a little and it wasn't quite so painful.

"Massage his muscles, yer not just brushing the dust off his hair, ye are sending oils through his coat. Ye are stimulating his nerve endings. Ye are encouraging growth.

"Oh, he seems to like it, look!"

"Aye, they all will."

"Mayhap I should use these on mi husband? Och nae!" They both burst out laughing.

A certain fair-haired guard had been out on patrol and had just returned, bringing his saddle back to the stables, he'd heard voices. He stood and listened for a moment, curious as to what the women spoke about. He chuckled quietly when he heard their conversation.

"This afternoon, we'll move on Lillian n' on the morra, ye'll ride."

It was a tack cleaning afternoon and Lillian's fingernails took a bashing. Although her sense of smell with the leather soaps had been fully restored! She loved it and kept taking huge sniffs, when she removed the lid off the tin to re-dab her cloth.

"Think I should use some o' this in his tub tae!" They both laughed again.

Just as they were packing up for the day, a guard wolf whistled at the women. Nobody ever admitted who, but another punch up started. This time there were four men involved. They hit each other in their faces and a black eye soon appeared, along with split lips and bruising.

"Why must they be so boisterous? It's unnecessary and quite demoralising for us women?"

"Pay no attention Caitlin, just men being men!" Lillian replied.

Once again, a fair-haired guard was close by, and he'd picked up the conversation.

Dreams and Plots

In Dunvegan, Lady Meredith's sleep had been very disturbed of late, and she woke up in tears, Stefan had his arms around her.

"Mered's, what's wrong love?"

"Oh no, a dream Stefan! What if it comes true?"

"Och, tis but a dream lass, whar appened?"

"It was over the top of me, here, on my bed!"

"Who was?" Now he paid attention!

"The Bean Nighe, or whatever that is, said a MacLoud will die!"

"Reet, well folks say she's a spirit love, an old lady who can travel between realms, although she does apparently carry these type of messages tae!"

"What if it's Caitlin?"

"Och nae, ye cannae think like tha love."

"I know, it just seemed so real!"

Stefan held his wife in his arms until she finally fell asleep, then he joined her.

"Rider approaching Sir!" Yelled a Dunvegan gate guard.

Laird Stefan came out to meet the rider and beckoned a Maid to ensure the messenger had plenty of food and drink as he nodded and took a letter from him.

"Thank ye lad, tuck in."

Laird Stefan walked to his study thinking it was a letter from Caitlin or Laird Fraser, but it wasn't! He opened the seal and sat down at his desk with a whisky in his other hand.

"Och nae, oh lord nae!" He was in shock.

The message was from his sister Isabelle. It brought bad news of his younger brother Hamish. In an unfortunate accident Hamish had taken a bad fall from his horse. The horse had broken a leg and flipped over, crushing him in an instant!

"Stefan, are ye alright love?" Meredith asked.

"Nae, nae, look ere." He handed the letter over to her.

"Oh no, this is awful news. I'm so sorry Stefan, anything I can do to help?" She hugged him.

Meredith knew he'd be very upset about his brother; he had been very close to him. But as each of his siblings got married, they moved away with their own family. Hamish left a wife and young son; they'd be heart broken. It would likely lead to a large funeral very soon and of course they would all attend.

Meredith wanted to ask if he had any word from Caitlin yet, but it wasn't the right time, so she saved her question for later. She also remembered her dream the other night when the Bean Nighe had visited and said a MacLoud would die! Now wasn't the time to discuss that either, she knew Stefan needed space, she'd be there, whenever he needed her.

In Castle Fraser a feast was about to start. Caitlin had gained a little more confidence in finding her way around all the endless corridors and her Maid Bella, had even shown her some short cuts. She had seen a hidden stairwell just in case the castle was attacked, and they needed an urgent get out through the tunnels, she also saw trap doors and spy holes which had been covered up with iron plates. Caitlin found all the history of the castle fascinating.

Bella had helped Caitlin with her hair and had plaited a thin top braid over her head. The sides and back lengths were left naturally long and curly. Her dress was brown coloured long skirt with a cream fitted bodice. It looked marvellous.

"Gosh, is that really me?" Caitlin looked in a long mirror.

"Aye tis n' yer vera beautiful Caitlin." Bella stated.

On the way out of her chamber, Caitlin fiddled with the top ribbons in her hair and walked straight into the fair-haired guard once again!

"Oh lord! I'm sorry, I wasn't watching where I was going."

"Och nae Lady Caitlin, twas my fault. I should be well used

to ye walking roond these passageways noo, we need more torches on the walls."

"Well, ye maybe right Sir." Caitlin nodded and shifted off to the main hall.

Caitlin's stomach flipped when she bumped into that man yet again. She didn't know why, but it seemed to happen every time he was close to her.

She walked into the main hall to find Lillian patting the chair next to her, beckoning her over to sit on the dais. Laird Fraser was in deep conversation with a few men when Lillian spoke.

"Oh, he's rather handsome isn't he Caitlin?" Lillian spoke quietly.

"Sorry, who is?"

"Tha fair haired guard over there, he's a braw physique tae!"

"Oh, what's his name, who is he, I keep bumping into him!" Caitlin asked.

"I dinnae ken but I will find out." Lillian was on a mission.

A Maid had answered her question and apparently his name was Ewan MacSwean. As Lillian whispered his name into Caitlin's ear, he looked over and caught her gaze, as she looked straight at him! He nodded politely.

"Oh, he seemed quite polite when I bumped into him earlier, smelled nice tae!"

"Oh Caitlin, how lovely!" Lillian was plotting.

When the food and drinks were about finished, the men pushed the tables back to the walls and the music struck up. Several couples began the dancing, some guards, and their wives.

"Lady Caitlin, may I have the pleasure of this dance please?" A man bowed in front of her with his arm held out.

It was Ewan! Caitlin took a nudge to the elbow as Lillian brought her back to her senses.

"Of course, she will kind Sir, come on, get up Caitlin!" Lillian shoved her out of her seat!

Ewan smiled and followed her along to the end of the dais, where she met his arm and gave a little curtsey of acceptance.

It was a slow dance, but Ewan remained honourable and kept a good space between their bodies. Caitlin was shaking and radiated heat.

"I believe, I currently have the envy of almost every man in this room Lady Caitlin!"

"Oh, only almost?" She replied.

"Aye Ma'am, ye cannae count the elders!" Caitlin laughed at his witty comment.

Ewan could feel the heat in her hands and her trembles, and he tried to make her feel at ease. He could smell jasmine, quite possibly her soap, he thought.

As they danced, her deep brown curls bounced around her

shoulders, her smile lit the room and Ewan saw how everyone was watching and admiring her looks, especially Lillian.

The following morning, Caitlin was just checking her saddle and mounting her horse whilst waiting for Lillian to arrive. They were supposed to be riding around the lake today and then into the forestry, she'd been looking forward to it all week. Ewan rode up beside her.

"Lady Caitlin, are ye ready?" He asked.

"Sorry? I'm waiting for Lillian. Erm, Lady Fraser I mean."

"Thas why I'm ere Lady Caitlin. She's nae feeling tae well, n' sent me instead, so ye would nae be disappointed."

"Oh dear, I hope it's nothing too serious! Mayhap I should go n' see her?"

"Nae Ma'am, she sleeps noo. Let's be off then!"

Ten other mounted guards rode with them although they stayed quite a way back as Ewan had planned to give Caitlin a full tour of the surrounding lands. At first things were pretty quiet, the lake was stunning though, so still like glass and it reflected the mountains.

As they approached the forestry, Ewan began to talk more and point out red squirrels and blue dragon flies and songbirds within the lush green canopy. The sun grew higher in the sky and shone down rays of light which softened the mood and made them both relax more. The ground was littered with moss and delicate fronds of bracken uncurling, tiny dew drops sat at its ends as it began to warm up and reach for the light. It was beautiful, fresh, and just what Caitlin needed as she sat tall in her saddle, beginning to enjoy the rather pleasant ride out after all!

Ewan noticed how the sun turned her curls into golden sparkles which lit up her face and how her smile appeared much more natural outside the castle walls. She thrived in the open air, outdoors, in among nature. He was proud to have such a beauty at his side.

The forestry opened up into heather moorland, the colour purple, and the smell it gave off reminded Caitlin of home.

"Come on, lets canter a while." Caitlin urged her horse on.

A short while later, as she began to slow the pace, her horse stumbled in a rabbit hole. It picked itself up though and regained its stance appearing uninjured. But not before hurling its rider off! Caitlin was on her bottom among the heather. She'd bounced quite gently really. Ewan immediately dismounted and held his arm out to her.

"Och Caitlin, are ye alreet?"

She was disgusted with herself! Embarrassed in front of everyone too. If only she didn't have her head in the clouds, she would have seen the darn rabbit hole coming, how foolish! She rose herself and shirked his arm away coldly.

"I'm fine. I can handle this horse myself!" She was angry.

"Lady Caitlin, I meant no offence."

Caitlin mounted quickly and trotted on as though nothing had happened. Her pride was hurt and what's worse, she knew she had snapped at Ewan. She would apologize later when she had calmed down. Secretly, her guard was up, and Ewan had seen this before, although he'd grown to like this mysterious stranger.

The ride back to Castle Fraser was rather quiet. Caitlin kept her eyes in front of her and Ewan didn't push his luck when he knew she was a little bruised!

Damage and Destruction

At the end of the week, Caitlin walked through the stables when she saw somebody working the horses in the enclosed area. She stood still, remaining in the shadows and watched. She recognized the man, it was Ewan. His shirt was missing! At first, she turned away but slowly curiosity and intrigue got the better of her and she turned around to see him fully. Although she hid back, he had spotted her watching him and he played proudly to his audience! He worked two horses at the same time, with one stick! Both horses followed the point of his stick and as he slowly dragged it out across the ground, they both bowed low! Caitlin was impressed but scurried away, not wanting to be seen.

Later the same afternoon, the sun shone really brightly, and it became quite a lovely hot day. Caitlin had changed and wore a simple cotton dress when she walked out into the walled gardens to see all the flowers out in full bloom. She could hear somebody chopping wood on the other side of the wall and decided to follow the noise. She'd spotted a small gate way that was overgrown with ivy leaves and wondered what lie beyond it. She pushed the gateway open whilst holding the vines back and glimpsed a small silver coloured butterfly. It was beautiful, she'd never seen one like that before and she wanted to know where it went and what flowers it preferred. But it had flown out of view. She had forgot about the person chopping wood and she came face to face with the woodman. It was Ewan and he was shirtless again! His muscles were out bathing in the sun's rays, his body glistened with sweat and his ribs were taught and layered. Caitlin paused in her tracks looking over his torso!

"Tis alreet Caitlin, I dinnae bite, in fact I'm quite friendly once ye get te ken me."

Caitlin stepped forward as he dug his axe into a log. She was unsure of these tingly feelings and why fate kept leading her to him.

"Lady Caitlin, would ye like me te show ye the old gardens?" He held out his arm.

"I didn't know there were any! I hope there are more of these silver butterflies, they're wonderful!"

Ewan led the way down a narrow cobble path, brushing leaves and twigs aside carefully. Ahead she could see a garden feature, an archway with a latticed roof and pale pink roses growing through the trellis work. Beyond the arch was a small room with curved seating. Ewan chatted calmly to Caitlin about titles and names to use and they were both happy using their first names only from now on. Caitlin began to relax. Ewan led her right to the archway and caught her hand at the door, he turned her to meet his eyes. She felt his breath on her face! Her stomach flipped again, just as Ewan tilted his head to one side and slowly brushed his lips against hers. Then he pulled back and met her eyes again. Caitlin was a little shocked but seemingly pleased! She placed her hand around his neck and brought him in closer, this time it was a little bit more than a brush and she kissed him. Whatever was happening, felt good!

"Och Lady Caitlin, I should nae ave done tha, I'm so sorry."

"Nae Ewan, tis erm, alreet! I did it tae." With those words, she hurried off.

The following few days were quiet, Caitlin was coming to terms with changes in her mind, as well as in her body. She knew her feelings for Ewan were growing more intense.

On Laird and Lady Fraser's wedding anniversary, they held another feast with music and dancing. This time, only family, close friends and important folk were invited. The meal comprised of lots of Salmon, their favourite food with salad vegetables with fruits and berries for desert. Caitlin's Maid Bella had told her that Ewan was a high-ranking guard, a warrior with an honoured position. She didn't think he had any family left alive hence the reason he probably joined the ranks as a youngster.

Caitlin wore a deep blue dress with a silver sash at the waist. Her hair was in a long plait behind her with a thin headband on top. Bella had stitched a tiny, delicate, silver coloured butterfly and had attached it to the top of her headband, Caitlin loved it.

When Ewan asked her to dance, she didn't hesitate to accept. Lillian clapped her hands and squealed in delight! She hadn't really been unwell that day they were supposed to ride around the lake, it was all part of her plan. A plan that seemed to have worked!

Ewan held Caitlin's gaze, their eyes silently doing all the talking that was needed.

When Caitlin danced with a few other guards later on, Ewan found himself a little jealous, although he stood tall and acted as though nothing moved him. Lillian saw everything, especially when Ewan puffed his chest out, as Caitlin swirled across the floor with other guards. She knew that the two of them were equally attracted to each other.

The days went by and every once in a while, Caitlin's and Ewan's paths would meet. They seemed to find ways to keep in touch. Be it a pat on the arm, or passing the horses reins, just split seconds of lingering onto one another's skin. A slow wink, a low nod, it continued.

One evening a fire broke out in the stables. Men rushed to and fro leading horses away from danger. Caitlin spotted Ewan, covered in soot, sweating, and running with three horses in tow! She realised he was risking his life to save these animals and shot off downstairs to help. The Castle was untouched, it had escaped the blaze, but the stables were an inferno and huge flames reached high into the sky. Smoke spilled out into the surrounding lands, blackening the views, and choking the inhabitants. A few nearby trees had caught fire and Ewan frantically chopped at them with an axe. Two other men helped, and they swayed the trees away from further damage, where it may spread to others. One of the Maids who stood watching said the flames reached as high as the heavens, others said she had drunk too much!

As the remains of the stable block dwindled to glowing embers, Lady Caitlin couldn't be found! Ewan went to look for her. He met Bella who was also searching for her, but she'd had no luck either!

"Men, I need twenty guards te search the castle, every room n' every corner fer Lady Caitlin. Ye others, I want ye te search the village n' lands aroond ere, set te it men, hurry!" Ewan stepped up and sent the men running.

"My Lady Lillian, I'm sorry I've nae yet bathed. The fires oot, but we've lost the stables n' we cannae find Lady Caitlin. Everyone's oot searching fer er noo." Lillian is horrified!

Laird Fraser orders a full search of the surrounding lands.

As dawn breaks, Ewan emerged from the lake, he'd gone to wash the smoke from his body. He is the Laird's best tracker, an expert in the field and he also knew the few pairs of boots and slippers that Caitlin owned. If she wore any of those, assuming she was taken, he would recognise them.

Searching the Forestry

Ewan set off in a direction different to the rest of the men, following a bare footprint, it appeared a fair size for a man, but it seemed to be deep set, as though this person was carrying something that weighed him down! He just had a hunch and his gut instinct told him to proceed.

The footprints changed as they led him deeper into the forest and becoming more wolf like and growing long claws! He didn't understand what was happening or if it was linked to Caitlin's disappearance, until he walked into a small clearing. In the centre were several large rocky boulders, one in particular, sat rather awkwardly on the top! He approached cautiously, his hand on the sword at his hip. On this upper rock laid a small silver coloured butterfly! The exact one which Bella had stitched yesterday for Caitlin. The boulder seemed to be covering something up, a well or a tunnel but he alone couldn't move it and his heart sank.

"Och nae, it cannae be! He roared for help.

It soon arrived too, in the form of Laird Fraser and fifty men, along with Laird MacLoud and a few more of his Fae friends, who had seen the fires blazing from a distance and came to help.

"Laird Fraser, where is mi daughter!"

The Laird updated Stefan and the Dunvegan team as well as his own men whilst Ghilly went for a walk about. Ewan stepped forward.

"Laird MacLoud, may I?

"You may."

"I danced with yer daughter last eve before the fire started, er Maid Bella ad made this fer her hair n' I ave just found it on the rocks. When I followed er tracks, they changed from human te a creature o' sort. I arrived ere n' fund this!" He handed Stefan the small silver coloured butterfly.

Ghilly returned and addressed Laird MacLoud.

"Sir, I've spoken wi the Forest Fellows, they will nae get involved as they dinnae handle trouble. But they told mi they'd seen the Beast o' Charred Forest here, last night! Its body thinned out te get doon tha hole, n' it had a girl in its grip! Tis rarely seen Stefan, but fer some reason or other it targeted Caitlin."

Stefan and a few men pushed the huge top boulder off its perch, and it rolled down to the ground with a thud. It exposed an old well with murky water sat at the bottom. Stefan dropped a small rock down and it plopped as it hit the water. Ghilly dropped a small, live fish down and the water rose to meet it, then emptied completely and within five minutes, it filled up again!

"Reet Kaylee n' Ghilly, can yer sift to the Kirk Yard n' look te the greying fer Caitlin? Return ere as quick as ye can. Aria, can ye n' Colby sift te ask Helga fer advice aboot this Beast of Charred Forest?"

Kaylee, Ghilly and Aria are Seelie Fae and helpful to humans, some can sift and others like Kaylee have visions and can look into grey mists for trouble or to locate missing people. It's come in handy in the past and the Laird hoped it would again.

Ghilly and Kaylee stopped briefly at Dunvegan Castle to update Lady Meredith and ask for something that belonged to Caitlin for Kaylee to hold onto. Lady Meredith handed her a doll from when she was a toddler, it unfortunately didn't give off any visions. In the greying, she saw nothing either, but she wanted to hang onto the doll for now.

Aria sifted back to Loch Ness, where she lived in a small bothy with Helga, an old Seer and friend of the MacLoud clan. Helga always claimed she spoke to Nessy and in return she left her seaweed for stews and potions, but nobody had ever seen her! Some folk thought Helga was mad, but her friends knew her better.

"All animals communicate Colby, be it on land or under water, n' I have heard from Nessy!

I'm afraid Caitlin is nae longer in the Noo! The Fiery Serpent tha some folks call the Beast, grabbed Caitlin. Tis born o' fire n' craves all things pure o' heart n' beautiful, tha drew it tae er ye see? It's taken er doon te the Lower Veils noo, tis nae good news lad!"

"But what can we dae Helga, we ave te bring er back n' how?" Colby asked.

"Mi dear, te fight a monster ye must dae so, wi another monster! But someone as te gan theer te fetch er back! Tha person must follow the beast's path!"

"Reet Helga, thanks, pls tell Nessy we are a bit rushed tedae n' we'll dip our feet next time!"

Colby and Aria sifted back to Charred Forest to inform Laird MacLoud. Helga's always been right in the past, so they trusted her word this time. The only question being, who would go? Who would dare, to enter the murky depths of the well, knowing it could lead to their demise?

"I will go Laird MacLoud. I will fetch Lady Caitlin back." Ewan stood tall and strong.

Stefan shook Ewan's hands and nodded at Laird Fraser in acceptance.

"Ewan, I ken yer a brave n' trusted man, but this is mi daughter, she's vera precious."

"I ken My Laird. I'm vera fond o' Lady Caitlin n' I will bring er back te ye safely Sir."

"Then so be it. Well done."

Other guards who had previously hung their heads low, not wanting to be chosen, all turned to look up at Ewan, thinking he was mad! But very brave and they feared he would never be seen again; this was his goodbye!

Rain clouds opened and the forest quickly became soaked. The ground grew boggy, and branches hung heavy. Very different from the sunny weather that Ewan and Caitlin had previously rode out in! Ewan knew the risks, he may drown or perish in some kind of mythical void, or even be consumed by creatures! Or he may actually find his love and bring her home. Either way, it was a risk he was willing to take.

With a rope he tied around his chest, the men lowered him down into the well and about three foot down, he saw the water begin to bubble and start swirling around. He knew his time was close, one way or the other. Ewan looked up at Stefan's face, then nodded and released the rope that held him secure.

As Ewan dropped into the unknown, the murky waters rose up around him. They pulled his body down deep, completely emptying the well! A few minutes later, it filled back to its halfway point and stilled. Ewan was gone!

"Thas one brave man ye ave theer Laird Fraser."

Confetti Petals

Ewan was rapidly yanked through a gateway and had already landed on his backside, on a hard rocky surface. He coughed to clear the last of the murky water from his lungs, as his eyes began to take in his surroundings. He was glad to be alive at least! His vision was a little hazed by the mists and smoky air around him, but he could hear something in the distance! It was a woman's voice, and she was sobbing! He hoped it would be Caitlin. He couldn't see much further than where he sat, so he had to follow his ears and stay alert in the process. Ewan began clambering over rocks and gritty terrain, passing some strange creatures that didn't appear to be bothered by his presence, but did look rather scary! They seemed quite docile like sheep as they grazed among the rocks for mosses and lichens. Their backs were covered in red spikes, their heads carried long spiral horns and they grunted deeply like pigs. They paid no attention to him as he passed by several, of what maybe a large flock, his hand on his dirk at all times. Ewan remained quiet, alert to all dangers but did wonder, even if he found Caitlin, how would they return?

The sobbing sounds were close now and Ewan, crouched

down behind a boulder to try and squint through the mists. He saw two figures, one appeared to be not quite fully formed and ghost like, the other was Caitlin! His heart jumped and he had to hold himself back, as he listened to their conversation. The dark ghostly figure was a spirit woman and she called herself the Bean Nighe!

Ewan wasn't aware this this was the same spirit that had recently visited Lady Meredith in her sleep and stated a MacLoud would die, she is an omen of death, a messenger.

"My dear, I am one of vera few, who can travel between realms, although we may only do this one realm at a time, remaining in each at least three days before moving on. I can tek ye te the next realm if ye wish, tis better than this lower veil."

Thats when Ewan stepped out from behind the boulders, clearly startling the two figures!

"Hope I can come along wi ye Ma'am?"

"Oh Ewan! Oh lord! Caitlin rose and embraced the brave man standing before her.

"Why did ye come? Ye risked yer life Ewan!

"Te find ye Caitlin, I ave te be near ye, I dinnae like it when yer so far away!" Ewan kissed her forehead.

The Bean Nighe wrapped a dark mist around them and sifted to another realm.

Minutes later, they woke up, sat on their bottoms! It felt warmer here and it was very bright on the eyes! There was no smoke or mist, everything looked clear once they both began to focus better. Caitlin looked over at Ewan, she noticed his fair hair had become white! He was also wearing a long loose smock type of dress! Minutes ago, he was covered in dirt and smoke! So was Caitlin and now her curls were white, and she wore the same long smock!

Ewan and Caitlin were now in the Silver Stream. It seemed to be a place of dreams and healing. It felt pure and enchanting and there were white horses roaming over the lush grass lands in front of them. The Silver Stream allowed those only pure of heart to roam upon it and everything became whitened, fresh, and clean.

All animals carried an element of this realm within them, and this was evident on the nearby lakes in the white swans, geese, rabbits, pheasants, and owls in the trees behind them. There were no fences, no walls or gates, everything was free to wonder, liberated, it worked well and created harmony in the lands.

"Only beautiful things can stay ere, tha includes ye two! Ye must stay a few nights, then I will come fer ye, te sift again, dinnae stray far from ere, ye ken?" The Bean Nighe said.

The couple walked a while, holding hands, watching the

swans on the lake. A nearby tree, an apple blossom, had an inviting grassy patch beneath it, they sat down and took a few breaths. The scenery was beautiful, and their white smocks gathered around their feet, as they wiggled their toes in the lush grass. Tiny petals gently fell from the tree in slow confetti storms, making them both feel special and relaxed as well as releasing a divine aroma. But they still held hands, Ewan wasn't letting her go again. It didn't take long before Caitlin fell asleep on his chest, he pulled her close and closed his eyes, falling into the dreamland himself. Everything was truly beautiful.

"Are ye ready? We're off!"

Caitlin had barely opened her eyes as the Bean Nighe sifted them both back to the Now.

Black Devastation

They were back in Scotland and somewhere along the Antonine Wall! It appeared quite ruined, and a lot of stones had fallen, but there were still small shelters every few miles. Ideal little bothy's if need be! Nobody else seemed to be around that they could see, however what they did see, shocked them. It was four beautiful white horses; they'd been tethered up outside the nearest stone shelter! They were from the Silver Stream!

"Caitlin, wake up, we're back in Scotland, although we are quite a way off home yet, but just look what has come through wi us?" Ewan said.

Caitlin saw the horses and was thrilled.

"Oh, I cannae wait te show them te mi Father, he'll love em!"

Ewan had told Caitlin of skirmishes and problems around the Antonine Wall in years gone by, neither of them wished to hang about there very long, so they carefully mounted the white horses and walked off towards the treeline. Ewan rode the stallion and Caitlin rode one of three mares. Their backs seemed to fit around the riders and gave them the most amazing comfortable seat, even without saddles! Both Ewan and Caitlin still wore the white smocks, but they were quite dirty now, and they had to pull them right up to be able to ride, this exposed their legs to one another! Ewan said when they stopped next, he would cut a small slit up the sides to rectify it.

"When we stop, we'll mek camp, n' I'll find us some food, we could be days from home yet Caitlin, I'm nae sure where aboots we are yet!

Caitlin kept smiling, she'd survived the Fiery Beast, the Well of Hell, the Silver Stream, yet being stuck in the Now with Ewan, would be the best adventure by far! Ewan wasn't sure of who owned the lands they were on either, but knew he needed to proceed with great care. Two figures in two white robes, with four white horses were rather conspicuous!

"Look, over theer Caitlin! There's shelter, come on."

The small bothy had only half of a roof and no door, but it did have a small hearth and a pile of sacks in one corner. Outside, were the remains of a building, but only one part wall stood now, it would be enough to give some shelter for the horses. They managed to find some grasses and bits of straw to feed them, although they seemed content enough just to rest for now! Ewan gathered a few bits of firewood and took them back to Caitlin who was busy shaking out the dust from the old sacks in the corner.

"I'll nip off n' fetch some supper, must be a few rabbits roond ere somewhere Caitlin, dinnae fash, I will nae go far."

Caitlin did start the fire and had gathered more logs, broken branches, and dried weeds for the night, when Ewan came back with two rabbits. He quickly dressed them and made a spit that anyone would be proud of, supper was cooking.

Caitlin enjoyed this simple way of life, she wished it could last forever, in reality things were never easy and rarely went the way she'd like them to go.

In Dunvegan, everyone had returned home. Laird Fraser had vowed to Laird MacLoud to keep searching for Caitlin, just as he did himself. None of them gave up hope. Lady Meredith worried awfully, her appetite lessened, and she grew quite ill.

"Mered's love, ye cannae worry like this, it'll de ye nae good. I ken ye worries aboot Caitlin, I ave em tae. It's been two months noo n' in three days' time, I'm riding oot again, deeper inte the forestry wi mi men, if ye get up n' eat well, mayhap ye could come wi us?"

"Oh alright, thats an offer I can't refuse!" Meredith rose, dressed, and began eating again.

"My Laird, may I?" A guard knocked on Stefan's door.

"Aye lad, go on."

"Sir, Nicholas wants ye in the stables, he said it wor vera urgent!"

"Reet, I shall be there in a moment, thank ye."

Stefan kissed Meredith's forehead as she brushed her hair, then left the chamber to go find Nicholas. He was a good friend of the Laird's and had been appointed to a high-ranking position some years back, Man in Charge of the Horse Breeding Programme. Nicholas has done a fabulous job; Stefan was very proud of all the work and of his horses.

"Och Stefan, tis the Black, he's vera doon. I fear he has nae long noo!"

The Black was Stefan's huge War Horse, he'd sired most of the mares over the years and produced some magnificent results, it was obvious his time was near.

Stefan approached his stall; the Black was laid down on his side. His body tired, dull not looking his usual self, age had taken its toll. Stefan knew in his heart, this loyal steed had worked so well, but now he needed to step into an eternal sleep. He wished the Black was young and vibrant once again, the Black's body told him differently.

Nicholas had cleared the stables of men in respect for his Laird and as Stefan sat down aside the Black, stroking his neck, he spoke softly. The Black seemed to relax when his master was near, he recognised his smell, his voice. Stefan wept, tears fell down his face and dripped onto the Black's cheeks as he slowly faded away.

"Thank ye my boy, fer all ye ave done fer mi, ower the

years. I dinnae want ye te go, but if ye need te tek ye leave n' rest, go, but ken ye will be tekin a part o' mi heart wi ye lad."

Stefan leant down and kissed the soft fleshy part of the Black's nostrils as they shared a final breath together. He'd gone. Stefan stayed a while, sobbing, his heart was breaking.

Hope

The following day, Stefan sat in his study, whisky in hand, staring out the window, feeling numb, lost in thoughts. Colby his Man at Arms and Second in Command knocked on the door. He wasn't heard. Colby knocked again and peaked through the door to see Stefan sat alone. He felt gutted for him and knew he was hurting.

"Stefan, brother are ye alreet?"

Stefan turned from the window and took another swig of whisky.

"Aye, I will be, tis alreet"

His eyes were reddened and glazed. Colby was glad his news wasn't bad.

"Kaylee's ere, she's ad a vision n' ye need te hear it brother!"

"Reet o, can ye bring er in?"

"Aye will dae, are ye sure yer alreet? Ye ken I'm always ere if ye need me?"

"Aye thanks Colby, just need time, ye ken."

Colby placed his hand on his brother's shoulder.

"Then tek yer time brother."

Stefan really wished he wasn't the Laird right now and

thought maybe it was time to hand over the Laird ship to his eldest son Dolan.

"My Laird, I've sin er! I held er doll again, kept it wi me just in case. I've sin er noo. She's back in the Noo, wi a man n' they both ave white hair tae!"

"Where are they Kaylee? Was it Ewan, are they well?" Stefan asked.

"Aye, all seemed well. I ken they're along the Antonine Wall but I dinnae ken exactly which part." Kaylee spoke excitedly.

"Well thas good news Colby. Be ready te ride at dawn on the morra, we'll tek a hundred men n' split off te scour the length o' the wall. Can ye set it up wi the men please Colby?"

The Antonine Wall spanned the breadth of Scotland in its day, marking the old borders. Many battles were fought around it and as each side breeched the wall, it fell into disrepair, later to be replaced by Hadrian's Wall.

At dawn a hundred men, mounted up and set off deep into the forestry. Ghilly and Kaylee went along with Sharoc and Hawk and Lady Meredith who rode beside Laird Stefan. It would be a long journey for all of them but hopefully a satisfactory one with profound results.

The Hawk

After what seemed to be days of camping out and trekking deeper into dense forestry Ewan and Caitlin had fallen asleep near an old wooden shack. The horses grazed quietly nearby, and Caitlin opened her eyes, it was only just daylight. She laid aside Ewan, his huge arms around here, keeping her warm and safe, her hand on his chest feeling his heart beating. Caitlin snuggled in tight to steal his body heat whilst she watched a bird flying over them. She thought of its freedom and its happiness as it flew by on the breeze and circled above, hovering over its prey. If only her life was the same, she was sure they would feel happiness and freedom, if they were left alone to do so.

"Oh! Caitlin sat bolt upright as Ewan quickly woke, hand on his dirk.

A rustling in nearby bushes brought them both to their feet quickly, their white robes now, grassy, and dirtier than ever! The bushes suddenly parted, and something leapt out! It was Janson! He took a flying leap onto Caitlin's knee once he recognised her, and she lowered herself to greet him.

"Oh, you softy, where's Kaylee, eh boy?" Janson wagged his tail in delight!

It was Hawk who had found them and led Janson's nose to their camp. Ewan and Caitlin quickly mounted up, hoping they could reverse Janson's tracks and locate their owner.

"Go on boy, find yer master, good lad, find Kaylee."

As they rode the whites they came to a slightly wider track and heard the sound of other approaching horses around the corner. Ewan had realised that whoever it was, must have been able to see Hawk circling above and possibly will have seen Janson running about in front of them too. Janson took off, he seemed to have found something, Ewan and Caitlin continued cautiously.

In Dunvegan village, the bells tolled. Its pattern meant the Laird Approaches. Laird Stefan and Lady Meredith led the procession on chestnut-coloured horses. Followed by Colby, Ghilly, Kaylee, Janson and Hawk, with a magnificent sight behind them! It was four stunning white horses, Ewan rode one and Caitlin another, although their riders appeared dirty looking in dress, the horses were pristine clean! A hundred men followed the lead group, and all were watching the whites in front. Ewan and Caitlin both had white hair now too, it only added to such a spectacle riding through the village and up to the castle.

Ewan MacSwean had held his word and brought Caitlin home to the Laird. Lady Meredith was really pleased but very tired now and went to rest. Nicholas had taken the white horses to a larger enclosure; he was keeping a close eye on them. Kaylee had informed Meredith before she went off for a nap, that she'd started seeing small silver-coloured butterflies in the apple orchard, one had even flown into the kitchen gardens around the herbs a few days back too. They were lovely and Meredith said she'd keep an eye out for them. Tina, Colby's wife was trying to study them and find out which flowers or herbs they preferred with a view to growing more. Maybe in the future wildflowers can have some kind of medicinal purposes, so all her work would be worthwhile.

Laird Stefan is very pleased with Ewan and what he did for Caitlin as well as returning with four exquisite white horses. It gave him hope. He still missed the Black but looked forward to spending time with the whites.

Stefan offered Ewan a high-ranking position within Dunvegan Castle and as Colby had his own family now, whom he wished to spend more time with, he was sure to reduce his hours of work thus allowing Ewan to fill in. Ewan came in at Third in Command, though Second in Colby's absence.

Stefan spoke to his eldest son Dolan. He wished to step down now and wanted to spend more time alongside his wife Meredith. Dolan had already learned a lot from his father, he trained well for years, since been eight summers old. He was ready to take his Father's seat as Laird, as soon as he felt the need to pass it over.

During a feast, one evening, Ewan led Caitlin to the Kitchen Gardens, it was dark, but the wall torches had been lit, giving off a warm glow and calm ambience. This was one of Caitlin's favourite places as she adored the smells from various herbs and healing flowers. There was a couple of the silver butterflies in front of them which settled down to drink at the side of the pool which Lady Meredith had made a few years back. Caitlin's eyes followed the butterflies to the water, then she noticed Ewan moving. She turned to see him crouched down on one knee!

"Caitlin, my love. Over the past few months, I've grown vera fond of ye. I've come te realise I wanna spend every moment I can, by yer side. Ye tek mi breath away lass, will ye mek mi the proudest man in Scotland n' become mi wife?"

Caitlin opened her mouth to respond just as one of the silver butterflies landed on her head!

"Ye see! We are back where we started, with the butterfly, tis a new beginning love!

Ewan waited.

"Aye."

"What? Ye agree te the butterfly or te mi....!" Caitlin cut him off with a kiss!

She may have her mother's looks, apart from the white hair, but she is so much like her father, especially in her mannerisms.

The Ceremony

Caitlin wore a pale lemon coloured dress with long draping sleeves. The fitted bodice was laced over a silver embroidered front panel. Her hair had been held up in a top knot, the remaining lengths left to naturally hand and curl down just below her shoulders. On the top of her head, she wore a slim headband, which had small silver butterflies embroidered on, one which her Maid Bella had been proud to make. She looked absolutely stunning.

Ewan wore his Fraser tartan kilt and a white shirt, his hair was tied back with a leather thong, and he donned a shoulder length of his new MacLoud tartan as a mark of respect, finished with a stag emblem pinned at the top. He looked very smart as he stood next to Colby, facing Father O' Brian at the head of the aisle. Seated within Dunvegan chapel were all his newfound friends as well as Laird and Lady Lillian Fraser, who beamed throughout the entire ceremony. Harriet and Dolan joined them and Elford with Maisie from Urquart too. Many village folk had come and stood outside waiting to see the newly wedded couple too, excitement was in the air. Folk from Boreraig joined them as their men folk were Pipers and they were all set ready to play.

Laird Stefan MacLoud proudly walked his daughter Caitlin

Mary down the aisle and gave her to her new husband. A Harpist gently plucked a few soft strings and gave a lovely backing mood to the spoken words. Time flew by and most of the women were in tears, dabbing their cheeks with handkerchiefs and holding hands with their husbands, it was a lovely ceremony.

"You may kiss yer bride."

Ewan hovered very close to her lips and breathed on Caitlin. She breathed gently back in acceptance, and he carefully met her lips. Caitlin was in heaven! She adored this man and looked forward to life alongside of him. Her Father had given them a large bed chamber to share once they were wed, it came with a Maid too, Bella, which also thrilled Caitlin. Bella and a few other Maids had naturally decorated the chamber, complete with hundreds of rose petals all over the floor and tiny silver-coloured butterflies on the huge four poster bed.

The crowds cheered as Pipers struck up and began to play, folks threw rice a flowers everywhere, the newlyweds, made off towards the main hall where a feast awaited them. The village had a hog roast too, compliments of Laird Stefan, everybody would have enjoyment for the event. The dancing drew on well into the early hours on the next morning.

Several months passed and Caitlin discovered she was with child. Lady Meredith suspected her time along the Antonine Wall may have been rather well spent, but now they were wed it was of no issue. Meredith was also pleased her daughter was close by and with her new husband who worked hard. Ewan and Caitlin were very happy, Stefan's Mother, Mary, was over the moon when she found out she was going to be a Great Grandmother too and Stefan had commented that he'd never seen so many women in the family, so busy knitting bairn's clothes! The wool merchant in the local market was doing a roaring trade.

As Caitlin's time grew near, her belly began to swell, and she blossomed. She never suffered a day's sickness either, unlike Lady Meredith who had awful day after day symptoms throughout her pregnancy. Caitlin just looked radiant, her skin and hair glowed. Ewan loved her newfound curves!

Labour had begun and Caitlin's waters broke. Gwen the Dunvegan Healer was at hand, and she examined her with Ewan present. Lady Meredith waited downstairs.

"Ewan Sir, Caitlin, yer bairn is breech, I ave te turn it, te be born. Ewan ye best leave n' ask Lady Meredith te come up please." Ewan kissed Caitlin's forehead and nodded with a smile.

Meredith entered the chamber, followed by Mary, Stefan's Mother and Bella who had fresh linens in her arms.

An hour later Ewan couldn't take any more and walked briskly back into their room, looking for any signs that the bairn had been born.

"Ewan, we cannae turn the babe, he's too low. But he cannae be born this way either. We dinnae ken what te dae!

"Och nae, Caitlin dinnae deserve this!

Ewan was distraught and Caitlin became weaker and weaker as time went by. She'd already lost a lot of blood and had become very pale faced; it was doubtful the bairn would survive this. Meredith rushed downstairs to Stefan and between all the Fae present, they managed to sift Helga, the old Seer, to Caitlin's bedside. Helga quickly examined Caitlin's stomach.

"Reet time is most important folks. I want everybody outa this room bar Mary, she can stay n' elp mi." Helga spoke up assertively.

Everybody left, closing the door behind them. Laird Stefan was in his study, handing out whisky to the men folk, they were all agitated and worried sick for Caitlin and the babe.

Mary and Helga talked quietly, they bow their heads in agreement and shake hands. Two older ladies, who spent years helping other people out, giving advice and being the backbone of the castle, they were now, two of the most important folk within the clan.

Silver Linings

A bairn was finally born! Ewan and Caitlin had a son, with white hair, seemingly none the worse for wear! Such a beautiful bairn. But Mary had disappeared!

Helga allowed Ewan, Stefan, and Meredith back into the chamber and as Ewan sat at Caitlin's bedside, holding his son, Helga began to speak.

"Caitlin is still vera weak. A mortal could nae ave carried oot this task, but a mortal wi Fae abilities could!"

They weren't sure what Helga meant!

"Mary has given up her life and her Fae abilities, te save the bairn! She passed the Tween n' noo lies peacefully in heaven. She asked me te pass this onte Caitlin."

Helga held out her hand and passed Meredith a brooch, it had a silver butterfly on its face.

Caitlin lay resting as Maids cleared up and freshened the linens. Ewan stayed at her bedside, still worried for his wife, he wanted her to wake up and smile again. Aria had sifted Helga back to their shack on the shores of Loch Ness where they spend a few minutes with their toes dipped in the water's edge, thanking Nessy, when Helga speaks up.

"Lassy, I ave te talk te ye."

"I'm ere Helga." Aria said.

"Caitlin n' the bairn, there were two o' em te return te the Noo, two bodies te save. Mary gave er life te save the bairn n' noo my time as come tae lass! I'm old n' Caitlin's nae lived yet. I've given what's left o' mi life, so she lives te look after the bairn. Yer welcome te stay, n' tek mi place ere though. It's been grand aving ye aboot lass n' I will always think o' yer, keep talkin wi Nessy, she'll tek care o' yer when in need. One more thing, I will nae leave

yer alone! I ave te go noo Aria, tek care." Helga walked into the Loch, deeper and deeper.

Aria was in floods of tears and unable to speak but as she rubbed her eyes to call out, she glimpsed a tail fin above the Loch's surface, one she'd never seen before! Helga was gone! Aria sat on the porch step of her little wooden shack, tears rolling down her face, deeply distressed and wondering how quickly it all had just happened. Through her tears, she noticed two figures walking towards her, just coming through the tree line. One a man who held the hand of a toddler and they were both Dwarfs!

"Good day te ye Ma'am, I was wondering if yer could spare some food for us please? I ave nae coin, but I'm willing te work te cover the costs!"

"Oh er, yes, nae botha, come in." Aria wiped her eyes, allowing her new friends to walk into her life.

Two private funerals were held. One within Dunvegan Castle grounds for Mary and another along the shores of Loch Ness for Helga. All the family attended including Ewan, Caitlin, and baby Arwen. Caitlin wore the pendant her mother gave her just before the wedding with a green gem set within and the silver butterfly brooch which had been left from Mary. She was very lucky to be alive. Ewan held the bairn as they stood looking over the Loch, thinking of Helga. Aria spoke up.

"Every time you see a cloud, wi a silver lining, think o' Helga. She'll be looking doon on ye n' watching the bairn grow!"

A tear fell down Caitlin's cheek, Ewan was there for her, holding her and supporting her. Meredith and Stefan watched on, always alert, always concerned for their children, no matter what their age.

Back in their chambers, in Dunvegan Castle, Meredith and Stefan had retired for the night and laid back on their bed.

"Te say we've stepped back a little Mered's, why are we so busy?"

"It'll ease out love, things will steady now, mayhap I can tek yer mind off things!"

"Aye well, if ye don tha black leather strappy, Scathach gear, ye definitely will! But what of our plans Mered's? I ken I'd like te breed those stunning whites that Ewan brought back, mayhap ye can elp me?"

"Aye well I could sit and sew all the bairns' new clothes, but I'd rather leave that to the Maids and Seamstresses really. I'd like te return to the gardens, maybe we could encourage more growth of those flowers the butterflies like? Although what I'd really like, is a trip out! Just me n' thee love! Do you remember riding up to Fancy Hill, camping? I could take cuttings of those flowers there!"

"Och love, I cannae forget tha, yer were amazing!"

"Well, you were pretty moving too."

"Reet, tha's settled then. We'll ride on the morra n' tek two o' the whites. I'll tek the stallion, ye tek a mare. We can leave em overnight, te roam, te graze n' well yer ken wor appens."

"Nae love?"

"Och, yer ken."

"Nae love, I dinnae ken, ye will ave te remind me!"

The Crystals of Life

Stefan and Meredith's life has calmed down a little now that he's handed the Laird ship over to Dolan, his eldest son. Although they are both now titled clan Advisers and sit upon the Council. Not elders, just yet.

Dolan and Harriet are doing well in their new positions, there's another bairn on the way. As with Elford and Maisie at Castle Urquart, they are one in front as Maisie had twins. So, with Caitlin settled too, all three of Stefan and Meredith's offspring are thriving. They have done their bit in life and have stepped back to once again, enjoy time with each other and what they like doing best. Stefan still sparred, mainly with Colby though and it was only ever for shorter periods of time, as his previously broken bones pained him and caused stiffness, especially in the colder winter months.

Stefan has always appreciated fine arts and has even tried his hand at oil paintings, but they are not his forte. After a few pointers from Aria on Loch Ness, he's taken a liking to pen and inks. Tina, Colby's wife, has even managed to use some flowers from the gardens to taint some additional colours for him to use too! Stefan's been drawing birds from the forest lately and they're quite good. Meredith copied a few of his drawings using embroidery threads and has been able to turn them into small tapestries. She has already managed to make some beautiful cushions for their chamber that are adorned with Greater Spotted Woodpeckers and Robins.

Sometimes Meredith puts her work onto the yoke or a pocket for clothing, the bairns all have birds on their chests now. Baby Arwen, Caitlin and Ewan's toddle has a lovely Blue Jay on the front chest of his smock.

Kaylee and Ghilly have extended the Orchard House, it's now twice the size, but it was small to begin with as they are both dwarves and didn't require all the additional heights. Dolan had agreed and allowed them to have additional lands too, now their harvest of potatoes and vegetables has doubled which is good news for all the clan and the villagers who barter their own goods, especially fruit pies which Kaylee loves the best.

Many different butterflies visit the Orchards regularly, it all helps with pollination. There are still some of the small silver-coloured butterflies about too and most folks end up saying things when they see them, such as 'Evening Helga' or 'Hello Mary.'

Aria's friendship has blossomed, and they have now become a couple with child. The dwarf Fae man, that her late friend the old Seer Helga, seemed to have sent, is called Brandon, he's about twenty summers old and the child, though not his, is Gaelum who is four summers old. There small hamlet was attacked by Bandits they think, and everyone fled, fearing for their lives, nobody has been found alive or dead as Dolan had led a guard out to check on his behalf. The village had been ransacked though. Aria had kindly taken them in, fed them and allowed them to rest up. Since then, they have never looked back and hit it off well. Brandon and Gaelum remained with Aria in Helga's old shack on the shores of Loch Ness, and all have grown to love each other.

Theres a travelling fair in Dunvegan village who usually only come once a year and Meredith would like to go and visit it but also browse the vast array of market stalls attending today and their size has doubled, due to the event. It's only a short walk away from the castle so Stefan agrees and takes along a small pouch full of coins. Meredith's quite excited to get out and about with her husband at last and she quickly spots a fortune tellers tent not far ahead. She insists they both go inside and have their palms read.

The lady in the small dome shaped tent is called Marianne, who is all dressed in brightly coloured silk fabrics with her head and lower face partially veiled. She called out to them as they walked close.

"Enter mi dearies, dinnae be afraid."

"Oh, come on Stefan, it'll be fun, what harm can it do?" Meredith pulled him into the tent!

"Noo then, sit doon folks, tek a breath."

Stefan grumbled under his breath, not very willing but wishing to please his wife!

"My dear, take my hands."

Meredith sat across from Marianne, between them, lie a small round table which had three crystals in its centre, all lined up, different colours it seemed too. They joined hands as Stefan folded his across his chest and just watched.

"Awe deary, I see so much pain! My oh my, how yer ave suffered! Awe a bairn tae, gone. I see an old lady, stiff in er bones, she's wearing a long grey frock wi a baggy mop cap n' pinny. She's telling me she's happy n' ye must keep smiling at the lambs' love!"

Meredith wondered if she meant old Elsie, her cook from Applegarth, it certainly sounded like her, but she remained quiet, not wanting to give anything away.

"Noo mi dear, come on, be brave!" She held out her hands towards Stefan.

He grumbled again, but grudgingly took the offer and looked at Meredith as if to say she'd be in bother later! Meredith just smiled back at him.

"Hmm, oh yer ave suffered tae! I feel pain, yer ave been injured, several times noo, ye must watch yer health n' keep them bones warm laddie! I see much love in yer family and there's someone called erm...Elga who watches ower yer kin, all are content."

Stefan smiled and thought mayhap she meant Helga, pretty obvious really.

"Noo then dearies, I've told ye yer past n' present, dae ye want me te tell yer ye future, it'll cost ye double the coin?" Marianne asked.

"Oh yes please!" Meredith answered quickly, not allowing Stefan time to say no.

"Reet well, ye two join hands n' give me yer free hand, lets form a circle around these crystals o' life. Look into the stones, see the colours." They did as was told.

"Och! I see a green gem, sumet so precious! Och nae, oh there's trouble brewing! I dinnae like this, och thas terrible!" Marianne released their hands and set about packing away!

"Marianne what's wrong? Did you see something? Please tell us what you saw, we need to know!" Meredith asked.

"Alreet, but ye may nae like it!" She sat down and replaced the crystals, joining hands again.

"When ye leave ere ye must act fast! Return home n' defend yerselves! Higher those walls, thicken those gates, gather all yer foods n yer people close! I see a monstrous battle coming vera soon tae! Ye ave two choices, flee noo or stand strong!"

With that, Marianne grabbed the coin and bid them farewell! It left Stefan and Meredith quite shocked but what she spoke about them as individuals seemed to be true. Why shouldn't they believe her as a couple?

They returned to the Castle and spoke to Dolan in the confines of his study.

"I dinnae ken if it will be true or nae son, but it will nae harm te strengthen out defences just in case." Stefan advised.

"I agree Father n' thank ye fer bringing this te my attention. We'll dae tha reet away n' I will dispatch a messenger te ride tae Castle Urquart tae let Elford ken, he can make his own mind up what he wishes tae dae."

"A wise choice son, well done."

Lady Meredith was worried for their lives and that of her sons.

Later that afternoon Kaylee brought two baskets of apples for the cook, then walked to the main hall to find her friend. She, being Fae, seemed to sense when something was amiss, especially when it concerned her closest friends and right now, she needed to find Meredith. They'd known each other for a long time, it was Kaylee who brought Meredith to Skye after meeting her at Loch

Ness when she'd come through the portal from Applegarth Farm on the North Yorkshire Moors.

Meredith was sat, supping whisky, staring into the flames of the hall's roaring fire!

"Meredith! Tis a tad early fer tha Missus!" Kaylee said.

"Awe lovey, I thought you might show up."

Meredith told Kaylee quietly, all about Marianne's conversation, Kaylee wasn't shocked.

"Dae ye remember when we first met at Loch Ness?"

"Oh yes, the early days, your endless bag."

"Dae ye recall walking miles, trekking around boggy moor land?"

"Yes, you froze and said we should divert around that moor, something bad was going to happen, yes thats right." Kaylee nodded.

"Oh! Do you mean? Oh, my lord!"

The date fast approached 16th April 1746, the Battle of Culloden. Thats what Kaylee saw in her vision upon that boggy land, all those years ago! Meredith was amazed and very worried.

Stefan found the women chatting and joined in.

"Dinnae fash love, we cannae dae nowt aboot it. If it comes, we'll support it. Though I'll be tae old te fight misen noo. I assume Dolan will lead a guard n' mayhap meet up wi Elford n' his guards tae. I could stay ere n fight, protect the castle, the women n' bairns from the village, there's many elderly folk ere tae. They'll all want te come inside."

"What if Marianne's wrong love?" Meredith asked.

"Well, that would mek my visions wrong tae, n' ye'll nae dae any harm strengthening yer defences any hoo." Kaylee added.

"I pray we can live through it Stefan."

"Aye as dae I love, as dae I."

"Reet, I'm off te Loch Ness. I'm gonna fetch Aria n' er family home. They can live in our extensions, there's plenty o' room fer us all. Then if owt appens, we can all come up tae ye

Mereds. We'll be stronger tagither Missus."

"Oh yes, thats a good idea. Are you going to spread the word amongst the villagers?"

"Well, we dinnae wish te cause a panic, they will ave heard whispers n' we ave the village bells te warn em early. Kaylee can ye let Ghilly ken, I will be sending lots o' Maids n' boys doon te the Orchard te gather all the food we can, from yer fields?"

"The men are working on the walls love, we'll all go down to help, a breath of fresh air will help us all."

That night, in their chambers within Dunvegan Castle,

Stefan and Meredith laid in bed talking calmly.

"Maybe we should move some of our treasured artwork away to the vaults love, even our green gems?"

"Aye, yer reet theer, we'll set off on the morra n' dae tha, good idea love."

"Are the tunnels all clear in case we need to get out quickly and are there boats ready in waiting? Enough for us all?"

"Aye love, although I dinnae think it'll come te tha but if we ave te tek a stand, the castle is strong, we ave enough food n' fresh water in the well te last a long time."

Stefan and Meredith laid on their sides, facing each other.

"Ye are strong love. We are strong. We can survive whatever life throws our way. I am yer husband n' I will always be by yer side. Noo, try te close yer eyes n' rest love. Think o' something beautiful."

"Oh, thats easy. Fancy Hill."

"Och, I cannae recall tha, mayhap ye'll ave te remind me love!"

Unbeknown to them, Bonnie Prince Charlie, the Young Pretender, had already landed in Scotland. The ways of clan life were about to change forever. Some folk would survive, but many others, wouldn't!

The End

Book 7

Caitlin Mary

The Laird & Lady MacLoud

Printed in Great Britain
by Amazon

36970432R00076